The Listener

Anthology of Short Stories.

The Listener
Anthology of Short Stories

James McEwan

First published June 2014

ISBN 13: 978 1508938972
ISBN 10: 1508938970

Printed by Createspace,
An Amazon.com company.

Also available on Kindle Amazon.com.

Contents

Acknowledgement

Acknowledgements and thanks to the Lanark Writing Group for their support and encouragement that inspired the publication of these stories into this form. Also deepest thanks for the feedback and comments from the community of readers and writers of shortbreadstories.co.uk, whose inspirational words I have truly appreciated.

The Listener.

This balcony is my studio and every day, and on warm evenings, I sit here with my eyes closed. The sunlight filters through my eyelids to create a canvas for my thoughts, in which I concentrate on the profusion of surrounding sounds, and I pick them out individually. They are like jigsaw pieces and I assign them a colour before placing them onto my imaginary painting.

When it seems there is a moment of silence I catch the gently rustling and soft movement of the breeze across my bare legs and face. I imagine the warm air as light blue and wash it across my screen. When a cloud covers the sun a shadow passes over my eyelids and I shiver slightly from the coolness of the air. This I paint as green, growing darker at the bottom of my landscape. I sprinkle the high-pitched chirping of the birds as yellows with red and blue that flirt a melody of songs back and forth along my picture. The soft cooing of the doves becomes two pink hearts on a branch and when I hear the sudden crack of wings in flight, I paint a flash of white in my sky.

'Will there be ice cream?' A child's voice interjects from below.

'Maybe, if Dad has time.' A woman replies. 'Look there's our car. You can ask him yourself.'

'I want vanilla with chocolate sauce.'

The sound of them walking below the balcony is rhythmic and solid until their path seems hollow. I hear their steps reverberate as they trot over a wooden

1

James McEwan

bridge, and I draw the echo as repeating lines of fading grey. In my scene I colour them hand in hand as they meander away, chatting of creamy flavours.

The lapping of water grows louder and I brush in a narrow stretch of reflecting silver with grey that curves on my horizon. Music, from a saxophone playing, bounces into the balcony and is accompanied by a melodic throb of an engine beat, and water splashing. My memory retrieves a barge, low in a canal, and I colour the hull pitch black.

'Hoy John, watch you don't fall.' Someone shouts.

'He's not listening.' Another voice replies.

'He's close to the edge. He'll fall.'

The saxophone leads with an upbeat jazz while the engine drums and the water splashes like cymbals. I hear a cacophony of sounds in delightful harmony. So I paint women in cocktail dresses and men in tuxedos dancing wildly to the music from an orchestra, who are all dressed in evening suits and bowties.

I feel the boat shudder below the balcony and its engine throttles an agonising roar, the water froths and bubbles. There is a lingering smell of diesel fumes, and the sounds of the music and throaty engine slowly fade. I didn't hear the splash of anyone falling, so I draw a white cloud of joy with happy notes that drift and dwindle away into silence.

I smile as a moment of peace hovers over my thoughts of the past, when I could walk and watch my children by the river. They would point out the fish basking in the shallows.

During dinner there would be stern discussions about the benefits of peas and red cabbage that were reluctantly eaten, or sometimes not. At bedtime the girls would giggle as we recited from their storybook the colours of the rainbow.

'Watch where you are going,' I screamed at them in the park one afternoon as we raced along on our bicycles. I was so concerned about them I didn't see the dog until it leapt onto me. I was knocked over an escarpment and landed hard on my back amongst some sharp rocks.

The Doctor said that my eyesight may recover and I might learn to speak again, but the nerve damage and paralysis will be permanent.

Once, lying in my hospital bed I had chuckled and spluttered as my daughter spooned soup into my mouth, she had been lecturing me about the healthy benefits of vegetables.

My thoughts were interrupted by a woman's voice from below the balcony.

'Look at all this blood. Did you fall?' She called out.

'No, I just came to look.' A young man answered. 'I've heard there was a fight here last night.'

He heard? No I've heard that voice before. I remember the evening when the action was loud and frightening.

He had shouted, 'Don't ever touch Susie again.'

Followed by the sounds of scuffling and punching. Then there was a scream of agony with a splash and frantic thrashing in the water. Silence.

'He deserved it,' she had said.

'Get rid of it,' he had said.

I heard a plop, a splash and the sounds of rapid steps that ran and died away.

On a new canvas in my mind, I had dashed the green of jealousy over a shadow and on its yellow face of pain I slashed some red. I painted the moon's expression aghast as an impotent witness, and like a spotlight over the stage of Shakespeare's Macbeth.

I may never see the view from my balcony or no longer be able to walk with my children by the canal.

But I live every day for my paintings prominently displayed in my mind. They are beautiful and full of colour. However, I now have a sad scene full of dark and tragic sounds. It hangs in my mind's gallery tagged to the voices of murderers.

If my nerves ever repair themselves, and I am certain, I will be able to identify them. However I need to speak to someone first and try to understand why, before I can decide what to do.

'Here's your soup Mum. It's lovely and warm.' My daughter, Susie, would always say. 'You deserve it.'

A Card From George.

Margaret covered the Valentine's card with the blanket on her knees. She must be going mad, a card from George, but we all know he's dead. Better not let Alfred see it, what would he say? Yet there are no roses, why? Where are the flowers?

She was sixteen when Alfred had bought her roses. Her first Valentine's, it was a Sunday. Yes on Sunday, they had walked round the lake to Kempinski's Café for hot chocolate and a slice of Black Forest Gateau, oh the cream. It had begun to snow so they stayed all afternoon and huddled by the log fire where they drank champagne. Maybe it was sparkling lemonade, but it tasted like pink champagne. Papa was annoyed when she got home. 'Gallivanting again with that Alfred,' he had snapped. Mama had given her a hug and put the roses in a Meissen vase.

'Are you ready Margaret?' He said, and turned the wheelchair towards the door. 'The sun's warm today.'

'Oh Alfred have you forgot? You always forget.'

'No Margaret I'd never forget our walks. Please don't start.'

'I'm not calling you Alfie, if that's what you mean. Where are the flowers?'

'The snowdrops are out, they're lovely and maybe we'll see daffodils.'

'Your friends would call you Alfie.'

'Now Margaret lets not talk about that today.'

'It's Alfred, I would tell them.' Margaret pulled the woollen blanket tight over her knees and legs. 'It's Alfred.'

He opened the French doors and came back to trip the brakes on the wheelchair, then he pushed her out into the fresh air. The path sloped from the patio and wound gently down into the garden.

'Look at the snowdrops, Margaret. It's like a carpet of snow.'

'Is it going to snow?'

'No, not today, can you see how blue the sky is?'

It had started to snow that day, when they stood throwing breadcrumbs for the swans. One aggressive bird flapped out of the water to snatch at the bread in her hands. Alfred had pulled her back. He felt so firm holding her, their noses touched and she blushed at the idea. Why didn't he kiss her, oh how she wanted to be kissed on Valentine's.

'In the sky, can you see them?'

'Oh Margaret. Look over there see the robin.'

'We must give it some crumbs. Did you bring crumbs?'

'If we go to the pond, we can feed the ducks.' He pushed the wheelchair out of the garden into the park. They heard the calling of the geese and watched the flock fly in a "V" formation like a compass needle pointing north.

'There they are, look can you see them?' Margaret said, and pushed her headscarf back. 'Can you count them? Have they all come home?'

'Yes they have all come home. Now lets find the ducks.' He pushed her along the compacted gravel path by the edge of the pond.

'Not everyone came home, you know.'

'Please Margaret not today, that was such a long time ago.' He positioned the wheelchair by the waterside and pulled the brakes on. They threw pieces of bread over the surface of the water and the Mallard's began swimming towards them. A black water hen dashed among the group grabbing what it could, the ducks flapped and chased it around in the water.

'You should have kissed me.'

'I did this morning. You know, when I helped brush your hair.'

'I wanted you to kiss me on Valentine's.'

'Look Margaret, there's a teal, we don't often see them around here.'

She touched the card under her blanket. Poor George he never came home. He had left with a big smile and had said, 'love you and see you soon.' But it was Alfred she loved. Why has he forgotten the flowers? She gave a small moan followed by a cough.

'Are you alright dear?'

'Yes, yes don't fuss,' she said and adjusted the blanket on her lap. 'Let's go up Berry Hill.'

'No, no it's too far away, besides the track is rough and too steep.'

'Come on Alfred, you said we'll picnic on Berry Hill?'

'Picnics, yes Margaret those picnics. That was sixty years ago.'

He pushed her across the grass and up a small hill to a viewpoint. He locked the brakes on the wheelchair and sat down on the bench. 'Isn't it lovely today?'

'I can't see the airfield.'

'No darling this isn't Berry Hill. Look there's a swan flying over the woods.'

'Just one.' She sat forward in the chair. 'Just one, where are the others. Can you see them?'

'No darling, just the one.'

'You said you were a pilot, but George said you were only a rear gunner.'

James McEwan

'You know I piloted the Lancaster bombers. Please Margaret don't, the war is over now.'

'Ice cream.'

'Ice cream?'

'You brought ice cream to Berry Hill, but George didn't like it. He said it was off.'

'Well it was. Imagine having ice cream during the war.'

She pushed herself up in the chair and tried to stand up. The blanket slipped from her knees and the card fluttered under the bench. Leaning forward to reach it, she collapsed out of the chair and started to laugh.

'What are you doing Margaret?' He helped her back onto the wheelchair and folded the blanket round her knees. 'What are you thinking about? Stay in the chair.'

'I want to run down the hill and feel the wind in my hair.' She started to giggle then coughed and spluttered. She took a tissue from her coat pocket and wiped her nose. 'That was fun.'

'Come on we need to get back.' He turned the wheelchair down the hill. 'We'll have some tea in the conservatory.'

'The card, get the card.' She pointed back to the bench.

He let the chair go and went back to look for the card.

'Alfred,' she shouted. 'Alfred. Oh Alfred.' She went rolling down the hill towards the pond.

'Hell.' He went running after the freewheeling chair. 'Margaret turn the wheels,' he shouted. 'Turn to the right.'

The wheelchair rolled on and she was laughing, enjoying the sensation and she took off her headscarf to let her hair catch in the wind.

They had once freewheeled down Berry Hill. She was on the handlebars, laughing and screaming then Alfred lost control of the bicycle on the rough track. They tipped over and fell into the long grass, she had grazed a knee. He wiped it with his silk scarf then kissed it. He had kissed her knee. She had blushed at her thoughts. He helped her up and their cheeks had touched. Why didn't he kiss her?

The wheelchair rolled on over the path then into the soft sand by the side of the pond. It stopped. The ducks came swimming towards her. She was waving her scarf in the air. 'Whoopee.' She shouted, and her cheeks were rosy red. This scared the birds, and flapping their wings, they scattered across the water.

'Are you alright?' He ran to her. He was gasping for air and sat down on the wet sand.

'That was fun,' she said and looked at him. 'You're getting old.'

'I'm ...just...as...old...as...you.' He got up and pulled the wheelchair onto the path. 'You could have ended up in the water.'

'Let's do it again.'

'Let's go home.' He pushed her along the path towards the garden.

'Spoil sport.'

They reached the slope up into the conservatory.

'Lets get back into the warmth,' he said, 'I'll make some tea and get your medicine.'

She stared out of the French doors. The medicine made her feel sick and she didn't want to take the pills. Alfred said they used tablets in the war, if they were captured they just had to bite into them. They had to keep their secrets.

'Here's your tea and some jam roll.' He put the tray on the side table. 'If you swallow the pills and then eat the cake you'll be fine.'

She looked at him. George had given her a card and it was her secret. She swallowed the medicine and took a bite from the jam cake, it was lovely, and so now her secret was safe.

'The children are coming later. We'll have some fish together.'

'Are the children alive? The house was bombed you know.'

'Yes Margaret, really it doesn't matter any more. That was before the children.'

The doodlebugs came out of nowhere. Alfred must have brushed the dust from her hair and held her tight. She had felt safe in his arms. But he had to go, since all the pilots were needed for the big push, and she mustn't tell anyone what he had told her. It was a secret. Why didn't he kiss her?

'No one remembers the house. They bulldozed it away,' she said and wiped her nose. 'What are we going to do?'

There was a knock on the French doors. A man in fawn overalls carried a spray of red roses into the conservatory and placed them on a side table.

'There you are Mr Anderson. Just sign here.'

He signed. The man left.

'See darling I didn't forget.'

'No, I knew you wouldn't.'

'Don't you think they are lovely? ...And...I rescued the card from under the bench.' He placed the card next to the flowers.

Margaret stared at the card. How could she explain, what should she say, would he forgive her? 'Yes they are lovely.' She smiled at him and reached up to hold his hand. 'Thank-you. Oh George, they are really beautiful.'

The Lady in the Bauble.

Now you two it's bedtime. Santa will only come when you're asleep.

'Oh Grandpa, tell us a story.'

Only if you both stay still, no jumping around. Come on now, settle under the blankets and listen. Let me tell you about Grandma's Christmas bauble.

It was a dark wintry night and we were all huddled together reaching towards a small fire, stretching our hands into the warmth. No one spoke because they were afraid, afraid if they had slept they might not wake in the morning.

'We'll wake, won't we Grandpa?'

Shussh, let me tell the story.

We heard singing from across the field. A soft voice that sounded so clear like an angel calling, "Stille Nacht, Heilige Nacht". Round the fire and in its dim glow I could see faces sink beneath their bowed heads. What of our families at home and all alone on Christmas night? Someone in the dark hummed the tune and then sang, "Silent Night, holy night". The singing became louder and the chorus travelled like a concertina along the trenches. The words harmonised in the frozen air, sounding like a choir from Salisbury Cathedral. Everyone lifted their heads up and began clapping as if electricity had buzzed around sparking good cheer. We were smiling.

Over the field, the lone angelic voice responded louder and then was lifted by a voluminous crescendo, a multitude of voices singing from across the field. We all hushed and everyone went silent, drawn to listen, "Schlaf in himmerlischer Ruh", (Sleep in heavenly peace).

'Was it angels, did they hear the angels?'

Can you imagine the whole world singing, everyone all at once? The night sky was bright with stars and the frosted ground on the field glistened. Yes angels were watching and had come to answer all our prayers, for peace on Earth.

A small branch with leaves had landed on our heads in the afternoon so I had stood it in the corner of our dugout.

'Like a miracle, Grandpa?'

Ha, yes a miracle. We decorated it as a Christmas tree with silver paper and on the top I put the golden bauble that your Grandmother had sent. She had wrapped it in some woollen socks tucked in a cardboard box along with some chocolate and shortbread. Imagine shortbread baked at home. Everyone around the fire had presents, there were cigarettes and small hipflasks containing whisky that warmed and cheered us.

'Grandpa, were you there?'

'Did you see the angels?'

Shussh, you two, listen.

In the morning we waved and walked across the field to where we had heard them singing. They stood up and came out to meet us. I gave them some shortbread and they gave us corn schnapps. I showed them pictures of your Grandma and one of them shook my hand. He gave me rye bread with wine and he even had some gingerbread with little sweet buttons.

A football was kicked into the air and then it started. They challenged us to a game and we played all afternoon until it became dark.

'Who won?'

They did, three goals to two.

'Oh, the angels won.'

That night we all felt safe and warm. I wrapped up snug in a blanket and before I slept, I read your Grandmother's letter by candlelight. I put her photograph next to the bauble on the top of our little branch, and saw how her face reflected and flickered in the golden sheen. She was beautiful and I imagined her dancing, she smiled as I watched.

I remembered her words at the train station, she had told me to take care and always do the right thing, please she had said, don't be foolish and make sure to come home. Come home safe.

During the night we all slept soundly like snoring hibernating bears.

Next morning, thunderous roars shook the ground and great lumps of soil were thrown into the air. Our football field was torn apart, earth and stones were sent flying and came crashing down along our trenches. I saw someone tossed skywards by an explosion, and when he landed the trench collapsed around him. I could only see his boots.

'Run, run, run,' everyone was shouting.

We ran along inside the trenches to escape the eruptions and kept going until we reached a reinforced shelter.

When the explosions stopped. We sat waiting, silent.

Someone shouted, 'gas, gas, gas.'

I pulled on my mask and took some deep breaths to blow hard and clear out the stale smell of the dank rubber.

'What gas, Grandpa?'

Mustard.

'Yuk I hate mustard.'

Shussh and listen.

I saw a lad opposite hugging the shelter support, and he appeared so far away through the bottle bottom lenses of my mask. Tears were streaking down through the mud splattered on his face. I shouted to him to get his mask on. He looked at me, then I realised he had dropped or lost his respirator in the scramble to escape the front line trench. I knew him. He was an Archibald and one of the baker's sons. Always do the right thing your Grandmother had said. So I took off my mask and pulled it over his head. He struggled against me, but I forced it on him until he sat down trembling. He was cowering in the dirt, and looking like a hideous rubber faced creature.

The bauble. I had to go back to the dugout and get your Grandma's picture and the bauble. Don't do anything foolish she had said, but I wanted to see her face and had to have her picture, it was everything. What would she say if I lost it?

'No ice cream for you.'

Shussh, listen.

I went back along the trench towards the front dugout where I had left the picture. It was raining and great pools of mud had formed sucking at my legs with every step. I crawled to look round each bend and was caked in the sticky mud like a chocolate and caramel tart.

'I like chocolate.'

Shussh.

I went through a gap in the broken dugout, it was dark, but I saw a tiny glitter of light sparkle from the bauble. There was heavy breathing, I wasn't alone, and all around it was as if bears were still asleep. Someone flicked a match and lit a candle. There were some of the opposition football players from the day before, and I smelt schnapps and gingerbread. My little packet of shortbread was still lying next to our makeshift Christmas tree with the bauble hanging on top, and the picture of your Grandma tucked beside it. Next to her photograph others had put their pictures of children, families and girlfriends. Miniature faces reflected off the bauble's sheen like little angels smiling. I reached over and picked up the shortbread and passed pieces around in the dim light.

Then the roar of eruptions started again and shook the dugout. Everyone huddled into the sides of the hole, they were mumbling, cursing and hugging at the earth.

I snatched the bauble, and Grandma's picture then I crawled out into daylight, into the mud and smoke.

'That's enough now, it is time you two were asleep.'

'But Mum, Grandpa is telling us a story.'

'Horrible war stories no doubt, really Dad. It's Christmas time.'

'No Mum, it's about angels.'

'Oh yes, and if you look into the baubles on the tree, you see Grandma. But all we can really see are our own reflections.'

'That's right Mum. Little angels.'

Karen's Halloween.

In the dark Karen sat by the front window and waited. She stared out into the night with her attention fixated on the garden gate. Clouds slid away like black curtains revealing the moon, and its white light lit her face, as watery images of her reflection shimmered along the wet slabs of the garden path. Now that the rain has stopped, surely they must be on their way.

The flickering of lights through the hedge caught her attention and, she held her breath. Dim lanterns cast shadows of a group that jostled towards her house, and they stopped at the bottom of the garden. A slow squeak of the gate announced their entrance.

'They've come.' She said and gasped.

Up the path came a green-faced witch with crusty scabs on her cheeks. Behind her came Jenny dressed as Wednesday, her face powered white and framed by jet-black hair. She glided past a Humpback, who shuffled and moaned as he picked his nose. A pirate wearing a black eye patch with a red scar across his face followed after them. He wore some plastic seaweed around his neck and used a hook to pull along a reluctant luminous skeleton that sucked its thumb and wore a woollen bobble hat. Behind them, Batman closed the gate that screeched against its rusted hinges. He lifted up and stretched out his cape as he ran to catch up.

Karen opened the door and met them. She wore a chiffon nightdress that fluttered in the wind. Her face

James McEwan

was as pale as new white bread, her eyes were red from
crying and her lips blue with the cold, but she smiled to
see her friends. She skipped forward and hugged the
green-faced witch.

'It's a ghost,' screamed Jean the little skeleton, who
dashed behind her brother's legs.

'Karen, you're bald,' said Paul the pirate. 'What a
great costume.'

'You came, O you came,' Karen said jumping up and
down. 'Quick, come in.'

Kylie the witch held up her jack-o-lantern to light the
steps, and the face on the pumpkin grinned, as the
group shoved each other in the doorway. The wind
rushed in and rustled leaves around their feet. Hugh the
Humpback sneezed and then wiped his nose on his
sleeve, he exaggerated his limping lope up the step.

'Lennie, why are you dressed as Batman?' Karen
shrugged. 'It's Halloween not super heroes.'

The door blew shut behind them with a bang.

'It was a birthday present,' he shouted and followed
them into the kitchen. 'Are you feeling better?'

'Yes. Mum said I'd eaten something dodgy.' Karen
said. She smiled at Jenny as they placed their pumpkin
and turnip lanterns on the floor to form a ring of
glowing faces. Kylie filled a kitchen basin with water
and placed it on the floor, and Lennie dropped in the
apples, from his pack, causing a splash.

'Don't make a mess,' Karen told him. She pushed
Hugh the Humpback to one side, and she knelt by the
basin to bite a bobbing apple.

'You do it like this,' said Hugh. He dragged a chair
over to the basin and kneeling on its seat held a fork in
his mouth. He aimed at an apple and dropped the fork,
the plop in the water meant he'd missed.

Meanwhile Kylie strung up a line and hung the treacle scones, soft and slightly warm. Jenny skipped over and laughed.

'Come on Jean, have a bite at a scone,' said Kylie.

'No I don't want too. She's a ghost.'

'It's just a costume,' said Paul her brother. 'Come on, have a go.'

'No.' Jean scuttled into the corner beside the fridge and sat on the floor. Only the luminous bones on her gloves were visible as she fed sweets into the shadow of her face beneath the bobble hat. She gave a snorted giggle when Batman pulled an apple from the basin in his teeth and water poured out from beneath his mask.

Karen screamed in delight at Hugh the Humpback, who gorged at a scone and treacle trickled over his face. Kylie swung the line back and forth just missing Jenny.

Jenny waved. 'Come on Jean,' she called.

'Paul, I want to go,' Jean shouted. 'You said we were going to Mrs Bradbury's for trick or treat.' She ran out of the kitchen into the garden.

'Karen, do you want to come?' said Paul.

'I can't, I'm not allowed to leave the house.'

'Will I see you tomorrow?' Jenny said and danced over to Karen.

'I should be better tomorrow.'

Karen waved goodbye to her friends, the ghouls, who ran down the path to catch up with Jean.

'Hey wait,' Paul shouted, 'what's the matter?'

'She's a ghost, you know.' Jean said as Paul and Jenny caught up. Jean dashed behind her bother and hung onto his seaweed. Batman ran ahead fluttering his out stretched cape, followed by the loping Humpback holding hands with the green-faced witch.

Next day Jenny stood outside her house, and watched the removal men load the lorry.

'Soon be finished Mr Radcliff,' said a sweating man.

'There's no rush,' Jenny's granddad muttered and wiped his face with a handkerchief. He stood leaning on the wall and looked up at the tall windows of the house. His eyes watered as nostalgic memories flooded his thoughts.

Jenny remembered she wanted to see Karen before she left. But no one noticed when she skipped off down the street as if floating on the autumn wind, and even Mrs Bradbury didn't wave back from her garden, where she was hanging out some tea towels to dry.

She followed a path into the woods leading down to a chestnut tree by the stream. She jumped and grabbed the rope that swayed from a high branch, and swung with the wind. This is where she would come with Karen to play and sometimes catch minnows in the shallow pools.

The ground was covered with reddish brown and yellow leaves that swirled around in the wind. Jenny picked up two mahogany coloured chestnuts that perhaps Karen would like.

She skipped along the narrow path between the brambles and the sandstone wall to the open grassy spot, where her mother had collected the pink-gilled mushrooms for soup. Karen thought it tasted disgusting and Jenny's Granddad had only taken one small spoonful.

Climbing onto the wall she saw Karen at the top of the slope standing next to a row of large stones. Jenny leapt down off the wall and a blast of a wind engulfed her in a swirl of leaves that rushed and tumbled up the gentle hill. The small whirlwind swarmed around Karen and then, the expired breeze dropped the leaves onto the ground.

Karen reached down and picked up the two mahogany chestnuts that had fallen by her feet and rolled them in her hands.

'I miss you so much Jenny,' she whispered, and ran her fingers along the letters engraved on the polished granite. Jennifer Jane Radcliff aged 12 years.

Granddad's Birthday Cuff Links.

Anne counted out her money from her little tea tin. It was Granddad's birthday tomorrow and she would surprise him with those fancy cuff links. The ones with the regimental motif on, since he was always talking about his adventures from his war days.

She had sold her *Bunty* Christmas annual to Sally, saved all of her pennies and even found some sixpences at the bus stop. There were also the half-crown and two florins that she had not spent on her holidays.

The thrupp-penny bits were in piles of four, the tanners in twos and the pennies in twelve. She added them all up to eleven shillings and eight. Some of the pennies were old and worn with Queen Victoria on one side but that didn't matter, she had enough for Granddad's present. It was a special day for him as he was going to be sixty years old, and Gran had said it was a great milestone in one's life.

She went into Mr Roland's antique shop and saw that the cuff links were still there in the display case.

Six months ago Granddad had shown them to her when they had been wandering around the shop. Afterwards, they had gone and sat in the park and fed crumbs to the birds. Where, in his croaky voice, he had told her all about his time with the Cameronian Rifles and having a Lewis gun. His eyes had watered and he kept coughing and choking, he had said it was the best time of his life, which was awful really since it was all about fighting and being in the war.

In the shop the cuff links were still in the glass case and only eleven shillings and six, she would have tuppence left to buy some toffee caramels.

'Yes you, don't be touching anything.' Mr Roland looked at her over the black frames of his thick glasses.

'Can I buy the Cameronian cuff links please?' Anne couldn't stop smiling. She had saved and saved, and here she was getting Granddad his special present.

'Has a wee lass like you got any money?'

She took a sock out of her school bag and tipped out the money onto the counter.

Mr Roland took off his glasses and looked at her.

'It's clean,' she said.

He pushed the coins around counting them up.

'There's eleven shillings and six,' she said and just grinned. She was going to wrap the cuff links up in some birthday paper that she had kept safe.

'This is old money.' Mr Roland swept them off the counter into a shoebox. 'It's illegal, you can't buy anything with these now.'

Anne took the sock off the counter and just stared at him. 'What about the cuff links?'

'Sorry, maybe when you've some real money.'

Her legs began to wobble and a knot tightened in her stomach. 'But that is real money.'

'No there're illegal coins. Don't you know it's all decimalisation now.' Roland frowned.

'I want my money back please.' Her lip trembled as she spoke.

'Get out.'

'I want my money back,' she shouted.

'Get out or I'll call the police.' He shouted back at her. He came from behind the counter grabbed her arm, dragged her to the door of the shop and pushed her out.

Anne ran up the street and kept running until she reached the park. She sat on the bench by the sycamore tree. Her knickers and socks were wet and she didn't want to go back to school, because they would laugh at her. She would need to go home now and get dry things first.

An old man was sitting on the grass and leaning against a tree watching her.

'What are you looking at you old stinker?' She screamed at him.

He took another puff of his roll up and shook his hands in the air.

Anne covered her face and just let out a long wail and sobbed. She won't have a present for Granddad on his special day.

'Here take this.' The old man offered her a handkerchief and sat down beside her.

Anne swiped it away. Don't speak to strangers in the park she had been told because of the molestation, whatever that was. Maybe it was like decimalisation. He offered her the hanky again. It was clean and smelled sweet like Granddad's tobacco so she took it, wiped her eyes and blew her nose into it. She looked up and saw how bright blue the man's eyes were and how his face was tanned and soft. He looked nice and didn't really smell. A robin landed on the grass and cocked its head towards them.

'Oh look, Mr Robin has come to see what all the fuss is about,' he said.

'It's only looking for crumbs.' Anne sniffed and wiped her nose.

'Here.' The man handed her a marshmallow he'd taken from his jacket pocket. 'Now what's this all about?' He leaned over and lifted her foot. 'I think you should take these off and let your socks dry in the sun.'

She let him take off her shoes and socks as she told him all about Mr Roland and the cuff links she wanted to buy. She liked talking to him, because he just listened and nodded. It was only the top of her socks that were wet and they had dried up quickly enough. She put them on again ready to go back to school.

'Come on,' he said, 'you need to be a fighter like your Granddad.' He took her hand. 'Let's go and get those cuff links.'

Mr Roland had his back to the door when Anne came into the shop. He turned at the sound of the chimes.

'You again, what do you want?' He snapped.

Anne held onto the old man's hand, she gave it a gentle tug.

'Look, why aren't you at school?' Mr Roland pointed to the door.

'I've been in the park,' she said. Why didn't the old man say something about the cuff links?

'What?' Mr Roland went to his shop window.

'I was in the park.'

'Get off to school and leave me alone.'

'I want the cuff links or my coins.'

Mr Roland looked through the window, up and down the street. 'I will not tell you again.'

Anne gazed up to the old man who mouthed scream loud. She took a deep breath and screamed as hard as she could.

'Stop it.' Mr Roland came towards her. 'Stop it.'

She held onto the old man's hand and kicked out at Roland's shins, he stepped back.

'Ok, Ok,' He went to the glass cabinet and fetched the box with the cuff links, that he threw at her.

Anne caught the box and left the shop holding tight onto the old man's hand.

'There you are now. Well done,' the man said. 'Tell your Granddad, happy birthday from Charlie McCabe.' He turned and walked away towards the park.

 A bell sounded.

She shouted after him. 'Thank you.' Then ran up the street towards the school.

That evening Granddad puffed hard to blow out the single candle on his cake. Gran had said that one flame was more than enough for him at his time in life.

He put the cuff links into his buttonholes. 'Aye Anne,' he said and hugged her tight. 'Thank you ma wee darling.'

'And happy birthday from Charlie McCabe.' She grinned.

He looked at her and started to cough, his eyes reddened. 'Charlie McCabe, how do know about him? What tales has your Grandmother been telling you?'

'Who is he Granddad?'

'Oh just a dear old friend. Aye he saved me from being shot once.' He took out his handkerchief that smelled of tobacco and blew his nose. 'Aye he just stood there to save me.' He rubbed his face and Anne took hold of his hand. 'Aye, poor Charlie, he had one of those big hearts,' he said and wiped at his eyes. 'No no, poor Charlie, he was shot right through that big heart of his, bless him.' He gave a loud cough, snorted and wiped his nose. 'Right then Gran, get cutting, Anne deserves a piece of cake.'

Next day at school Anne learned all about decimalisation and the new money as it was called, which didn't become legal tender until after Christmas. She warned Sally about Mr Roland, and what happened when she bought Granddad's present. However, Sally

didn't believe the story about the old man in the park
and in any case she had said, molestation was only what
boys did.

Lost Lambs.

Mary heard the front door bang shut. She rushed to the kitchen window and saw her daughter Jessica, who was early for a change, crossing the farmyard, and in plenty of time for the school bus. Usually Jessica would wave but this morning she just flicked her hair from her eyes and strode on towards the lane.

What an argument they had last night about her old school skirt, the one she had since she was fourteen. She had spurted and grown so quickly that it now exposed her legs far too much above the knee.

'Oh Mum you're such an old fashioned fuddy-duddy,' she had grumbled, 'it doesn't matter nowadays.' She had stamped her feet and then, after some frustrated tears, capitulated and sulked in her bedroom for the rest of the evening.

Mary smiled because her daughter seemed perky this morning. She does look so neat and tidy, and although her new pleated skirt and blazer, with its school motif, were a size too large for her they should last until she finishes high school.

Mary took a deep breath and exhaled a long sigh as she watched Jessica adjust the strap on her leather satchel.

In the farmyard the family collie ran up to Jessica and she ruffled the dog's ears.

'Come on Bob.' She patted the collie's head as they crossed the yard.

'Bye Dad,' she called and waved without looking at him. She went skipping down the lane with the dog trotting by her side.

When he heard his daughter's voice, Gordon stopped splitting logs, and he straightened up to see her going towards the bus stop.

With two sharp pulls he tightened the straps of his dungarees, and then bit out a splinter from his thumb. Yes, perhaps he should really wear those gloves that Mary had bought him for Christmas. He lifted the axe above his head and with a long swing slammed it down to split through another log.

Back in the kitchen Mary sliced a freshly baked loaf and tasted the soft bread. It was good but not quite the flavour she wanted. For months she had tinkered with her grandmother's recipe trying to reproduce the springy texture she had remembered from her school days. When she was young the idea of visiting Gran would make her salivate for fresh bread, thick with salted butter and home made strawberry jam. There was no secret about the ingredients so perhaps it was the baking process that Gran had kept to herself, or maybe it was the type of wood she had used to heat the oven. In her grandmother's days they used different fuels in their cast iron cookers, but which was best? Was it charcoal or wood? Could it have been the hard wood that burnt slowly giving off a constant heat? She had asked Gordon to chop up some of the seasoned beech logs, piled against the wall at the bottom of the garden, as they might be the answer to her problem.

'Has Jessie cheered up a bit this morning?' Gordon said as he came in with a wicker basket full of split logs. He placed it next to the Rayburn stove. The cooker was warm, and an aroma of fresh baking emanated from the oven.

'Don't call her Jessie. She's Jessica and she's sixteen today.' Mary sliced up the remainder of the loaf. 'You know … quite the young woman.'

'So you keep telling me.'

'What do you mean?' She laughed and put the plate of bread onto the table, and went to fetch his breakfast from the bottom oven.

'What's up now, why only one egg?' He groaned and slumped into his chair. 'I've been milking since six. Look, there's plenty in the trays.'

'They're for the shop, and well … I need some for baking.' She tugged at the tea towel in her hands. 'I'll make some porridge if you want?'

'No thanks.'

'It's because … well… some of the chickens are missing. Maybe there's a fox about.'

'A weasel more like, there aren't any foxes left in these woods.' He cut his sausage, stabbed at the pieces with his fork and dashed them into the egg yolk as he ate. 'Call this living off the fat of the land. Mario's always had a great breakfast, … remember.'

'Well this isn't Mario's.' She threw the tea towel towards the draining board, but she missed and it landed in the sink.

They heard the dog barking, and a Royal Mail van drove into the farmyard.

'I'll go,' Mary said and picked up the box of loaves wrapped in baking paper and the tray of eggs.

'Morning Mary how's you?' The postman took the bread and eggs. He passed her a bundle of letters with the *Times.* 'You'd know it's no' my fault if I run over that collie dug. He snaps at the tyres. Ye know ye should tie him up.'

'Never mind that. How's Susan?'

'She's a hardy lass and just fine.' He grinned and told her all about Susan before driving off.

The collie dog followed Mary into the kitchen and went straight to its blanket in the corner.

'Susan's home from hospital,' she said and sat down. 'It's a boy.'

'Another boy eh. Is that what they wanted, eh?' Gordon said with his mouth full. 'It's all they talk about around here, breeding.'

'We should visit on Sunday, and I'll take them a cake.' She shuffled through the letters. 'Ah ha! Jessica will be pleased. Her friends from London have remembered.' She pushed the large envelopes to one side and gave a white embossed one to Gordon. 'It's for you.'

He tore it open and read the letter.

'At last,' he shouted. 'It's from the bank in London. I've been offered the position in Singapore.' He finished his tea in one long gulp.

Mary let out a slow sigh. The collie dog came forward from its blanket and pushed its head forward onto her lap.

'Are you going to accept?' Her heart beat faster. 'Are you?' She stroked the dog's ears.

'But Mary, it's what I'm best at, Merchant banking. Farming's hard, and I've given it a go and …'

Her lips tighten and she narrowed her eyes.

'I'll think about it,' he said.

'Well don't think about it.'

'It's mucky work, at least the bank pays.' Gordon reached over and placed a hand on her shoulder. She shrugged him off.

'You promised, no looking back.' She stood and went to look out the window. 'Remember, what we agreed.'

'Oh Mary, we'll see,' he said, 'I need to check on the lambs.' He got up and strode to the door. 'I didn't see the sheep in the top field this morning. Come on Bob,' he called. The kitchen door blew shut behind them.

She sat down with her cup gripped in both hands. The noise from the bang of the door subdued and accentuated the silence. She looked around the kitchen, at the Rayburn, at the yellow daffodils in Mum's old vase, and at Jessica's new green Wellington boots by the door. She loved the smells of fresh baking and all the musty odours from around the farm. This is home, not some modern flat in Singapore. Who wants to leave this countryside for a foreign city buzzing with traffic and full of busy people rushing around? She would have to kowtow to Gordon's work colleagues, and chat with their anonymous wives or partners, as everyone is referred to these days. Strangers.

Mary telephoned Susan.

'Hello it's me.' Mary sat down by the dresser. 'It must be nice to be home. How's the baby?' She continued, 'Malcolm, that's a strong name for him … almost seven pounds … yes okay then …see you on Sunday.'

She picked up the *Times* lying on the table and out of habit turned to the business section with its company updates. What was she doing? She doesn't work with the HSBC research department anymore. Rolling up the paper tightly she threw it onto the pile of logs in the basket. Why doesn't Gordon get the *Scottish Farmer* like everyone else? It might help to concentrate his mind on farming instead of thinking about the financial state of the world.

Mary paced around the kitchen. What would it take to convince Gordon to stay? Perhaps she should rally support. She telephoned her mother.

'Mum, how are you? … No, no…yes everything is fine, its just that the bank have offered Gordon a post in Singapore … I know.'

Yes, Singapore is a beautiful city, but she would miss the farm. This is where she belongs, walking among the green fields, prickling her fingers from collecting blackberries along the hedgerows, and riding her horse through the woods.

'No Mum … I hope so too … I'll just have to convince him … see you tomorrow then.' Mary put down the phone. If they left for Singapore, would they ever come back?

She had made the right decision to get out of London, a decision she had wished she had not left so late in her life.

There had been a tube strike on the day Mum called with the bad news, so she had to walk back to the flat. The pedestrians along the streets appeared like peripheral blurs outside her bubble of sadness. The worries about her father's illness were replaced with tears, and if only she could have been there, but suddenly it was over. Did it matter any more? She had gazed at the clouds dotted in the sky above the multi-storey offices as she walked, and when she had stopped at a crossing, the traffic fumes triggered her into a coughing fit. She had gasped in desperation for air and held a tissue to her face to avoid the sooty exhausts. It just seemed so difficult to breathe in the city, it was then she had decided; of course it mattered. She wanted out of London and back to the fresh air of the countryside, back home to the farm.

The farm had been left empty for a few years after her father's funeral, and they'd rented the grazing to neighbours for their horses and sheep. Her mother had moved into a lovely bungalow in Peebles to be near her friends. They came up from London whenever they could to see her, mostly at Easter and Christmas.

Mary found it hard leaving after those visits, because the farm would provoke deep emotional memories and longing for the countryside. A clear sky was always a joy when she was growing up and when walking to school. She had missed the buttercups that grew in the low meadows and the bluebells that carpeted the woods, which were so radiant in the spring and early summer. The fun times she had chasing the butterflies and avoiding the bees amongst the Dog Rose along the hedge, and listening to the calls of blackbirds and the sound of the skylarks that appeared as tiny specks in the sky. The familiar early chorus of the countryside would follow her all the way to the school gates, and occasionally she would pick some daffodils in the lane for the teachers, who always placed a vase of fresh spring flowers in the classrooms.

'They're not about.' Gordon shouted as he burst in to the kitchen. The collie followed in behind him. 'The gate by the woods was opened, they've got out.' He rushed over to the telephone.

'I've just made some tea.' Mary poured out two cups.

'Jack ... what? ... It's Gordon ... yes I know ... my sheep have got out ... I know ... have you seen them?' Gordon put down the phone.

'Have you checked the woods?' Mary offered him a cup.

'Yes, the woods.' Gordon shook his head at the offered cup, and rushed out into the yard, the collie chased after him.

Mary sat at the table to drink her tea and smiled. Gordon was very excitable, just like the first time they had brought baby Jessica home to the farm to meet her Grandmother. He carried the infant all round the house then together they toured the garden and out to the stables to see the horses, afterwards to the byre to meet the cows and the chickens in the yard.

The economic recession was a turning point in their lives and the City in London reacted with a sweep of redundancies. She had grasped this opportunity of being unemployed and convinced Gordon that their futures together should be a healthy life in the countryside.

Perhaps her Mum had not sold the farm because she knew how much it meant to Mary, and intuitively kept it as an incentive to encourage her home and be nearby again.

She grimaced then chuckled at how much they had argued over the costs for the renovation of the farmhouse and the choice of new roof tiles.

'They have to be slate,' she had argued with Gordon.

'Tuscany red Rosemary tiles are better,' he had said, 'besides it gives the place a more rustic look.'

They had agreed on grey slate. The decisions they had made about rebuilding the ruined barn into a garage and the choices of landscaping the garden were just right, and made the place look almost new.

However, there was little left from their redundancy packages once the farm was restocked. The Ayrshire cattle and Texel sheep had brought life back into the fields, and it was as if her childhood had regenerated itself.

'Oh Gordon,' she sighed. She loved him dearly, but he had not appreciated the physical effort needed and complained often of being so tired. However over the last year he became fitter, even smiled more often, and looked so much better with his handsome outdoor tan. Once, standing up in his mucky dungarees after checking the sheep's hooves for foot rot, and with his hands bleeding from scrapes and cuts, he had burst out in a fit of laughter.

'Look at the state of me,' he had said, 'this is awful.' He then caught hold of another ewe and turned it over to inspect its feet.

Jack from the neighbouring farm helped and had shown him how to treat the sheep by splashing them through the insecticide dip to protect them from mites and blowfly.

'There's nothing like getting mucky to experience the farm,' Jack had laughed when he showed him. 'How else can you appreciate the value of honest work?'

Mary finished up her tea. She picked up the letter from the bank and read through its offer of a post in Singapore that threatened everything she had dreamed about. How was she to convince Gordon that a city life was no longer for her?

She gathered up the dishes from the table and slammed them into the kitchen wash- bowl. One of the plates broke into pieces.

Through the kitchen window she saw a van drive into the courtyard, and she fetched her purse and went out to meet it.

'Hello George,' she said, then pulled her cardigan tight and folded her arms.

'Top 'o the morning, Mrs Frazer,' George said. He opened the van doors as she crossed over the yard. 'What do ye fancy t'day? I've really nice plaice filets, Arbroath-smoky and kippers. The trout and salmon are in season. All local stuff, fresh from the Tweed.'

'Just three pieces of plaice today, thanks.' Mary pointed at the dents along his van. 'What's happened?'

'A float full of sheep cut the corner by the woods.' He grimaced. 'The bugger hit the side of the van. The bug ... sorry, he didn't stop.' He selected the fish and slapped it onto some greaseproof paper. 'But I got his number and I've called the polis.' He passed the wrapped fish to Mary. 'I would count your lambs if I was you.'

After putting the fish into the refrigerator Mary changed her cardigan for dungarees. She went out to the yard and looked across the fields, but couldn't see Gordon. Perhaps he had gone beyond the woods to find the sheep and the lambs. She went into the stables.

'What if I gave Gordon a choice; either home on the farm with us, or Singapore on his own.' She spoke to her mare as she rubbed her hand down its nose. The horse nudged back at her, she picked up a brush and started to groom along its back.

'What would Jessica think?' She didn't want a repetition of the sulking they had when they left London.

'I am not going.' Jessica had kept saying and stomping around the flat. 'What about my friends?' she had nagged on and on, 'and in any case I don't speak Scottish.'

She had locked herself in her room. But with some gentle words from Mary through the closed bedroom door and coaxing her with ideas of seeing her grandmother more often and owning a horse had eventually brought her out beaming with excitement.

'There you are Chestnut, all brushed down,' Mary said to the horse and went to fetch some rye hay from the back of the barn.

When they first moved into the farm, Jessica had made a point about the isolation. What exaggeration, they were only a short walk from the village and only ten miles from Peebles. It was hardly the end of the world as she had suggested. It didn't help when she found an enormous spider in the bathroom and had grumbled about creepy crawlies.

'How could anyone get used to being suffocated by the smell of silage and manure?' She had often grumbled.

At night she was convinced ghosts haunted the house, apparently they walked on the roof and tapped on her window. Gordon cut back the branches from the adjacent beech trees and cleared out all the crows' nests. The haunting stopped.

Jessica's attitude changed when she was given the lead part in the school play, "Cinderella". Her classmates liked her, and she had settled in quickly enough making new friends, in particular with the twins, Tom and Clare, who lived within a ten-minute walk on the neighbouring farm.

But then again she was young and in many ways was still a city girl, who would probably adore the bright nightlife of Singapore.

It might be two against one, so what would convince them to stay?

She lifted a bale of hay from the top of the stack and behind it was a hen sitting on a nest.

'Well then, what's all this?' She moved another bale to one side, there were two more hens clucking away on their nests. 'So this is where you lot are hiding? I'll better get you back into the hen house.'

A hen came out from a gap between some bales followed by a group of yellow chicks chirping and stumbling over each other.

'Wait till Jessica gets home and sees you lot.' She searched around the barn and found all the missing hens, and herded them back to their compound. She checked the perimeter of the netting fence of the hen run and tightened up the loose sections.

Gordon came running across the yard with the collie by his side.

'Did you find them?' She looked at him then turned and locked the hen house door.

'No. I'm going across to Jack's to ask him ...'

'George said his van was hit by a lorry full of sheep.'

'George?'

'The fish-man, he told the police.'

'Right then, I'm off to see Jack and then to the police.' Gordon got onto his Quad bike and drove off towards the lane.

'I've found the chickens, by the way.' She shouted after him.

Later in the afternoon she was beating chocolate butter icing in preparation for the eggnog gateau baking in the oven. She counted out the sixteen candles together with their little plastic holders.

'Hi Mum,' Jessica said as she rushed through the kitchen door. 'Just going to get changed.' She ran up the stairs. Within minutes she was back down in clean jeans and her favourite floral blouse.

'What's for tea, Mum?'

'How was school? Oh, there's some cards for you.'

Jessica tore open the envelopes, and stood the cards up on the kitchen table.

They heard a car and Jessica dashed to the window.

'Oh good it's Tom. He past his driving-test today and is taking me for a drive. Isn't that great.' She dashed towards the door and shouted, 'I'll be back in time for tea.'

'No, no wait, where're you going?' Mary called after her. She looked out the window to see Tom laughing as he opened the passenger door of the Land Rover. His fresh complexion, curly brown hair and strong healthy stature were so like his father, Jack. Perhaps the new Barbour jacket he was wearing was a reward for passing his driving test.

'Well now, well, well, perhaps the city girl enjoys country life after all.' Mary chuckled.

*

'So Gordon, what's it going to be?' Mary wanted to know as she started to clear the kitchen table.

'I'm not going to boarding school.' Jessica rattled the teaspoon inside her cup. 'Could I not stay with Tom and Claire?' She kept stirring the spoon in her half empty cup of tea and glared at her father, who was eating a slice of gateau.

'No one is going to boarding school,' Mary interjected. 'Are they Gordon?'

'What about university and, how often will I see you?' Jessica was interrupted by the telephone ringing and lost the race as her father got there first.

'That was the police,' he said. 'They've found our lambs. Isn't that great.' At the mention of lambs the collie sat up in the corner and cocked his ears forward. Gordon went over to the stove to put on another log, and turned back to the table, both Mary and Jessica were looking at him.

'What?' He shrugged his shoulders. 'You found the chickens and we've got the lambs back. Is that not fantastic?'

'You just threw your *Financial Times* in the fire,' Mary said and stood staring at him.

'Yes, I know.' He coughed. 'I've decided, I am committed to this farm and I am not going to Singapore.'

'Oh Dad.' Jessica leapt up, knocking over her chair, and hugged her father. 'This is the best birthday present ever.'

The collie started to bark at the sudden excitement, and wagged its tail as it ran round the kitchen table and jumped at Jessica. The sudden burst of joy released a well of tears from Mary, who took a deep breath, before she joined in the commotion by dancing around in the kitchen.

The Accountant.

Norman stared at the clock, willing time to fly. He tapped his left foot in coordination with the movement of the second hand, every moment an eternity. He touched the brown satchel that rested against his chair. It contained his sandwich Tupperware box, a blue plastic thermos and a novel, John le Carrié's *Tinker Tailor Soldier Spy.* During his lunch break he indulged himself in the world of secrets, spies and intrigue. Exciting escapes from the rows and columns of figures representing the dealings and profits within the world of commerce. This was his world; expenses, taxes, interest formulae, calculating, counting and listing reports. Dull and so dull.

Norman polished and replaced his glasses, he brushed his hand through the wisps of hair over his bald patch, only five minutes to go and he will be on his way. His heart was racing. He stroked the satchel, he had bought something special and it was in his bag.

He need to go the toilet so folded up the files on his desk and took them to the central cabinet.

'Are you alright Norman?' The girl by the window said. 'Does it still hurt?' She twisted in her chair and crossed her legs, there was a flash of white lace. He gave a small sigh, the glance of white panties distracted his attention and he rubbed the back of his neck.

'What are you doing later?' She was smiling at him.

'I'm fine,' he said and closed the cabinet drawer. 'Must get on. Train to catch.'

He went to the bathroom and looked into the mirror, one side of his face was slightly swollen even though the anesthetic had worn off. He needed a drink.

The girl had asked what he was doing later but then that's all they did after work, drink in the Counting House and make arrangements for the weekend before they went home. He agreed to have a drink with them once and that was a mistake. He had never wanted to join in their gossips and opinions of X factor and max factor, so he had just sat there and absent mindedly fidgeted with a beer mat. They then decided to draw straws as to who would take him home, he beamed red and hated himself. He had wanted to leave. Calm down they were only joking, they had said. Not that he would have gone home with any of them, in any case.

Back at his desk, he sat down and ducked behind the partition. He lifted his satchel onto his knees. No one was looking. He reached in and touched them. Soft silk French knickers, so smooth in his fingers and with a sensational touch of the satin on the bodice, he slid his hand over the ribbed supports and tugged at the laces.

He had bought them on the way back from the dentist. He was beaming and could hardly speak, when he had stroked them in the shop.

'Don't worry, there's no need for embarrassment sir,' the sales girl had said, 'lots of gentlemen buy them for their sweethearts.'

They were perfect and will be a snug fit. He looked up at the clock, it won't be long now.

Carol held the gold locket with its inscription close to her cheek. Her eyes were watery. Those soft green eyes that had attracted Brian when he was swimming in the sea, they had entranced him and captured him like a mermaid, he had said. She put the locket down beside the silver frame on the dressing table. In the picture, Brian was wearing his diving equipment on the first day they had met. The hot white sand had trickled through her sandals on their wedding day and she had squinted in the sunlight as he kissed her on the beach. Together, they had found the locket in a sunken Spanish galleon, cleaned it and had put in the cropped photograph from their wedding day. She dare not look and gave a long drawn out sigh.

Ten years had past since she had sat by his hospital bed, praying he would pull through. She wanted to die with him when they insisted that she give permission to switch off the life support. Since then, as she mourned, her green eyes had formed a steel grey shade, and now with one cold stare she would hold the gaze of any man until he quivered for release.

She brushed her dyed auburn hair and pulled it back into a ponytail. He'll be here soon. What will he like? Once she was a model that tantalised the fashion designers, and later with Brian's money she had set up a health spa and fitness club for women. An excellent income, but nevertheless a woman needs a hobby.

She picked up the tarot cards and spread them across the table, then dimmed the lights to create a mystical mood. She was ready and stood to examine her choice of costume in the mirror that covered one wall of the bedroom. Rubbing her hands over the soft leather, she eased out the creases over her flat stomach and firm bottom. The black cat suit revealed every contour of her body and emphasised her figure, still that of an eternal young model. On the corner of the table she rearranged her business cards, they promised full satisfaction or money back – no quibbles. No one had yet complained, simply because she was good, very good.

The ring of the doorbell prompted her to pull on her feline mask and she adjusted her hair back into its ponytail. With slow deliberate steps, on her stiletto calf length boots, she crossed the wooden floor and opened the door.

'He- l –l o,' the visitor said 'are you...' He stopped unable to complete his words. The anonymity of the eyes through the feline mask held his stare. A pulse of electricity swept through his body that tingled every nerve in the back of his neck.

'Come in,' she purred. 'Let me take your coat.' She leaned forward and kissed his cheek. 'Have you brought them?'

'Yes, there're in my bag.' He shifted his view to an object on the table.

'The bodice and the knickers?'

'Yes'. He stared at the table.

'Let me, Norman.' She took off his glasses and brushed back the wisps of hair over his baldness. 'Would you like me to help you put your knickers and bodice on?'

'Oh yes, please.'

She went across to the table and picked up the leather harness with its solid rubber phallus. 'Do you like it? Do you want me to wear this, Norman?'
'Oh yes, Miss Kitty, … oh yes please.'

She Blew Me A Kiss.

The girl rushed into the compartment and she dropped into the seat diagonally opposite, to my right by the window. She looked out and down the platform as if searching for a friend or relative, who might wave. But no one was there. Rapid beeps preceded the closing of the doors and the train smoothly moved off.

Her red hair was tied into a ponytail. Freckles dotted her nose and her cheeks were clear and soft. She wore a white blouse covered by a tight tweed jacket, a short skirt and her light green tights stretched down her legs into the ankle boots that matched the light tan of her satchel. Early twenties.

A woman directly opposite from me shook her *Hello* magazine and we exchanged glances. I returned my attention to the crossword. Four down, the colour of jealousy, five letters. Green and isn't that also the colour of envy?

An increasing volume of a ring tone from a mobile telephone had the girl rummaging in the satchel. The woman opposite lowered her magazine, tightened her lips and shook her head as she glared at me over her glasses.

Six across, slight discomfort in the organs. Ten letters, try irritation.

The girl placed a notebook on the seat, before retrieving her telephone from the bag.

'Where are you?' She spoke into her mobile.

The woman rustled her magazine to a new page and turned sideways.

'Well get the next one.'

What kind of boyfriend misses meeting this girl, with bright blue eyes? Seven down, an inferior assistant, three letters. Slave, no that's five, try cad.

'Carol, you always say that.'

Not a boyfriend then, perhaps it was just a friend with a lame excuse, and who had probably slept in.

'No its Ok, I can wait in Starbucks, you owe me.'

The woman stared through her glasses at me. Well don't listen I telepathically glared back and clearly you should avoid Starbucks.

'He did what?' The girl stamped a foot on the floor. 'Oh Carol he didn't. ... He did.'

The woman took a deep breath and lifted her hand to cover an ear. Perhaps she doesn't want to know what he did. Three down, something rare or unusual, nine letters. A curiosity. What was it he did?

'But, is he coming with us? ... He is.' The girl stamped her foot again.

The woman folded her magazine and shifted in her seat, she crossed over a leg and accidentally kicked me. Ouch that hurt so I smiled at her and rubbed my shin.

'I'm going to ask Mark along, if that's Ok?' The girl on her mobile looked at me.

The woman opposite mouthed sorry.

'No harm done.' I said and return to my crossword.

'What do you mean?' The girl glanced at the woman and then stared across at me. She shifted the mobile to her other ear and turned to look out of the train window. 'But Carol he's good looking and ...'

Eight down, having no choice eleven letters. Involuntary, now that's an interesting word.

I watched the girl's reflection flicker in the window where her face appeared contorted by the diffractions of light and passing background.

'No no Carol … Mark said what?' The girl stomped both feet.

Oh dear, what did he say? Perhaps Mark is too good looking or perhaps he is a two timing selfish sort. The woman turned a page in her magazine and a picture, of George Clooney with a beautiful woman in an evening dress, smiled at me. Oh how the celebrities live their lives.

'I never want to speak to him again.' The girl hugged the satchel resting on her knees.

So many times I've heard that before. Nine across intended to mislead, six letters. Deceit, yes we all fall for the same old excuses.

She started to laugh. 'I know … you should have seen him.'

So clearly he made a fool of himself, somewhere.

'I know what an idiot.'

So you're better off without him, he can't be trusted and you'll find someone else. Twenty-four down, influenced by proximity, ten letters. Attraction, what does she find attractive?

She looked at me. 'Who should I invite?' She said into the mobile.

Why not me? I smiled.

Next clue: four across, an impractical person, and eight letters. Idealist.

'No Carol, he's too old for me.' She looked out of the window.

She's noticed me, but surely we could try. The woman turned over another page of her magazine and I saw Michael Douglas with Catherine Zeta-Jones holding hands. It works for some.

'I don't care, I am not going to ask him.'

She has no sense of adventure, I am sure if she got to know me, we'd be a perfect match.

'That's what you think.' She spoke into her mobile and looked at me. 'I'll tell you later ... later I said.'

The train announcement called out, 'the next station is Central Low Level.'

In a connecting glance with the girl I instinctively felt a mutual desire and a perception of more to come.

'No way,' she said. 'I'll meet you in Starbucks, bye ... bye.' She returned her mobile telephone into her satchel.

Sixteen down inspired with foolish passion, ten letters. It can only be infatuated.

The girl shouldered her satchel and left the train. Rapid beeps preceded the closing of the doors and the train started to move off.

Someone knocked on the window from the outside. It was the girl. She frantically pointed at the seat where she had left her notebook. I grabbed hold of it. The top window was jammed and I rushed to the next compartment. The girl was running along side the train and I threw the book out to her. She picked it up, smiled, waved and then she blew me a kiss.

'Oh really,' the woman said as I returned to my seat. She shook her magazine to a new page. Renée Zellweger was smiling at me from a picture, as if she knew why the girl blew me a kiss.

The Orphanage.

'You are in my bed,' she said, 'you're in my bed.' She giggled.

The voice woke him. He lifted his head off the pillow and saw the outline of a small girl by the window. She sounded familiar, like some one he had known. When?

'Sally?' he said. Surely it's not, he must be dreaming. Perhaps this girl is in the wrong room.

'I'll get into the bed with you, then,' she said and chuckled. 'We could snuggle up. You like that don't you.'

He propped up a pillow and sat up. In the semi-darkness the girl was like a transparent shadow against the curtains and her face was obscured. He switched on the sidelight by the bed and, on his travel alarm, saw it was three-o-clock. He looked up but she was gone. He slumped out of bed and eased the door open to the en-suite, empty. It must be his tiredness playing tricks with his imagination. Sally had been a lovely little girl and a mischievous child, but it was such a long time ago. He looked in the wardrobe and under the bed then behind the heavy woollen curtains but there was no sign of her.

Out through the large bay window, he noticed the half moon above the trees at the foot of the garden. It shone like a spotlight down on the children, who were chasing each other by the rhododendrons. He spluttered, coughed and drew hard to close the curtains, ripping one side off its rail.

Back on the bed he began wheezing as his angina thumped inside his chest. These apparitions were new, flashbacks to his time in the orphanage.

He should have realised immediately when he read the address and the directions. The orphanage had been renovated and was now a modern Hotel with a conference centre. That afternoon beads of sweat had rolled down his back when he drove up the gravel drive. Did he hear some children playing? He had wanted to leave and should have turned around and left, but it was too late, he had been seen.

The whisky bottle was half-empty and he shook it to check the level. He hadn't drunk that much, surely not. The doctor advised him to stop, but what does he know? It was just the one glass to relax and to help him sleep. He pressed out a blue tablet from a small foil sheet, and to mask the bitterness of the Stelazine, he washed it down with a mouthful of the peaty malt whisky. He needed to sleep and didn't want to think about his speech in the morning. He switched off the light and settled back into bed.

'Shall I massage your back, Mr Grimshaw?' The small voice teased him.

He sat up. The naked girl under the duvet was rubbing her hand inside his pyjama top. She tugged and played with his hairs around a nipple.

'You promised to help me, if I made you happy.' She giggled. 'It would be our secret, you said.'

'No Sally.' He switched on the sidelight. 'Why now…?' He was alone. Sally was gone. He dared not switch off the light and took another large mouthful of whisky, directly from the bottle. He leaned back and closed his eyes.

The ringing, from the alarm clock, alerted him to the time, it was seven-o-clock. He must have dozed occasionally, but still he had been awake all night.

Someone was knocking. He eased himself out of bed and put on the hotel dressing gown before he opened the door.

'Room service sir, you ordered breakfast.' The waitress carried a tray and placed it on the table. 'Shall I pour your tea sir?' She looked up. 'Oh dear what happened to the curtains?' She walked across and pulled them fully open. 'I'll have to fix them later.'

'Yes, please.' He sat on the bed.

The waitress stood and stared at him.

'What is it?'

'John, its you, John Grimshaw,' she said.

'Sorry, no I'm David. David Donaldson.'

'It's me, Mary, don't you remember?' She went to him. 'But you're dead, there was a suicide note. You drowned.'

'Please, can you just go?'

'Something was upsetting the horses in the stables, that's where I found Alfred.'

'Alfred?' He started to drink his tea. 'What do you know about Alfred?'

'See you do remember. I held him in my lap and I thought a horse must have kicked him.'

'Please, just go.'

'He kept asking for you. Get Mr Grimshaw, he kept begging me.'

'What do you want?'

'All the girls loved you Mr Grimshaw. They were so excited when you promised.'

'Promised?'

'I had an inkling it was you, when I saw you arrive. I just had to be sure,' she said, 'first Alfred, then the fire, then … but they never found your body.'

'I don't know what you're talking about. Please go. I have a busy morning.'

'All the girls were locked in the room ... screaming.' The waitress closed the room door and stood against it, blocking the exit. She stared at him. She knew. 'Do you know what they were screaming?'

'Look it has nothing to do with me, now please just go.' He finished his tea. 'Do I need to call the manager?'

'They were screaming. No Mr Grimshaw, Mr Grimshaw please, Mr Grimshaw help us...you promised.'

He got up off the bed and went to her. He stroked her cheek and smiled.

'Now look, Mary, what are you thinking?'

She grabbed at the door handle to leave but he forced his hands around her throat. He tripped her, she grabbed at his hair as she fell and then went limp. Her neck was broken, her eyes remained set in a fixed stare.

He threw his suitcase on the bed and opened the wardrobe door.

'Alfred?'

'You hurt me Mr Grimshaw,' Alfred said. He was stood beside the hanging suits.

Mr Grimshaw stepped back and fell over a chair. A pain surged and tightened in his chest. The pills. He had to take his medicine. They were on the side table. He crawled round the bed, he was wheezing, spluttering and then his heart gave one last thump.

He was walking alone in the woods with the warm sun shining onto his face, it was so peaceful, and as if he was floating free from a heavy weight. The ground was covered with golden, brown leaves and there was an occasional rustle from where blackbirds foraged in the undergrowth.

'Mr Grimshaw, Mr Grimshaw,' Sally shouted and came running down the path towards him.

Behind her followed the other girls from the orphanage, they were shouting, 'you came. You came to save us.'

'Have you found us a mum and dad?' Sally took his hand. 'You promised. We are all waiting for our new families. You promised.'

He looked down at her, at her happy mischievous face.

'What is it?' Sally said. 'Did Alfred tell, did he spoil everything?

Mr Grimshaw looked up the path and he saw Mary and Alfred, who were stood watching him. Smiling.

Ellen.

The tall rosebay willow herb and nettles blocked the path to No 52 Mortonhall Way and the key, still in the lock of the blistered door, was disintegrating with rust. Ellen stood on the pavement and stared up at the dilapidated building. There was a baby crying, and its sound was muffled behind the sandstone walls. Rainwater, like teardrops from the cracked gutters, splashed over the steps and as if knocking, bounced onto the door. She shivered and pulled her coat collar up to protect her neck from the constant Edinburgh haze. Its cold drizzle was an omnipresence that saturated her clothes, and permeated through her skin into the essence of her soul. She was drowning, drowning in a world of depression.

'Someone. Help,' she mouthed the words. 'Please help me.' Her voice was in a paralysis and unable to form coherent sounds. She turned to walk away but the crying from behind the walls became louder. It was as if the building had pleaded in a child's voice, it called out to her, 'Ellen … Ellen … Ellen.'

She screamed. A silver cord formed to connect her navel to the door. It was strung with water droplets that bounced off into the air as it pulled tight and tugged her forward up the path. Naked, she grabbed at the cord with both hands to jerk herself free, but the cold wind hit her from behind. She was engulfed in a black mist from which hands emerged, to hold her and push her, forcing her up the steps. In the wind, the nettles thrashed and whipped as if to punish her. They beat her naked legs with their tough stalks and the acidic stinging hairs blistered her skin. The rosebay purple headed flowers hung wet as if ashamed and shook their disapproval with the breeze.

The door opened and the cord dragged her into the hallway where she tripped and fell. The flowery wallpaper tore itself off the walls and pounced onto her. The thorns from the roses stabbed her skin until blood became smeared over her body. A cold baby, covered in afterbirth and with its umbilical cord tight around its neck, was kicking on her chest, its small fists and arms hitting out at her, its eyes wide in panic. The door slammed behind her with a loud bang.

Ellen grabbed at the pillow on her chest and screamed.

'It's only me,' her mother spoke softly. 'Sorry. The draught must have caught the door.'

'I had a terrible dream.'

'I've brought you some tea.' She sat on the edge of the bed. 'You don't look so bad today. How are you feeling?'

'I don't know.' Ellen sat up. 'Just as awful.' She felt a warm dampness under the sheets. 'I think I've wet the bed again. Sorry.'

Her mother took a blue medicine bottle from her housecoat and poured some of the dark liquid into the tea and offered it to her. Ellen felt something slide off her legs and pushed the cup aside to grab and throw the bed covers back. A small bloody partially formed foetus lay between her knees. She screamed, scratched at her face, pulled her hair, and shook.

'Oh dear,' said her mother. 'Quick, I'll call the doctor.'

She rushed out of the room and down into the kitchen. She chuckled and laughed as she picked up her mobile and called for an ambulance. She read the label on the blue bottle on her hand, "Pennyroyal Essential Oils."

'Oh Pennyroyal our cradles you do deceive,' she muttered and put the bottle to the back of a top shelf. 'If only I knew about its effect twenty two years ago.'

'Are you sure this is the right place.' The driver of the ambulance spoke into his radio. He looked up at No 52 Mortonhall Way where the tall rosebay willow herb and nettles blocked the path, and the key, still in the lock of the blistered door, had disintegrated with rust

My Fear of Light.

My captors chattered constantly outside the small building and although I did not understand their language I listened. Any raised tones or excitement would cause me to lean back against the wall where I squatted, and I'd stare at the steel door.

The evenings cooled the building and when the voices became silent I felt safe enough to try and sleep. From my position in the corner I would crawl, feeling my way along the wall, to my bed. There, I would lie on the flattened cardboard boxes where I could stretch out my cramped legs. I would sip water from the plastic bottle that I kept tucked under my trouser waistband. My blanket was a large towel, in which I wrapped myself for warmth despite its fetid smell.

I would drift in and out of sleep and dream about my daughter Alexia. She was waving to me on her first day off to school dressed in her new uniform. Then, images of headless bodies holding her hand, as she skipped along side, would shock me. I would bolt upright fearful and listen.

My only comfort was from sipping water, and that outside it was still silent. I was alive and to be reunited with Alexia was my only concern in life, my thread of perpetual hope.

Constantly waking and checking for what I used as an alarm clock, a chink of light through the cracks in the breezeblock wall. In the morning, I would then go to the corner behind the metal door and slide the lid off the pit that was my toilet. My trousers were ripped and the sleeves of my shirt had been torn off in my first desperate struggle with my captors. What dignity I had left was preserved by the loneliness in the semi-darkness. I stunk and was engrained by layers of filth from the dust, and my hair was matted from constant sweating. A fresh splash on my face and neck with water from the bottle was my attempt at normality. It was a ritual of self-respect that gave me the psychological strength to face what I knew was to come.

I would squat in the furthest corner from the door and calm myself with rhythmic breathing, and listen for movement outside. Under the morning sun the dry atmosphere in the cell gradually became stifling hot. I waited and watched the ray of light from the crack in the breezeblock slowly shift over the dust and detritus of the floor. I calculated it would happen any moment now, and my sweating fear mixed with the rancid odour from the toilet pit.

With a crash, the steel door burst open and the blinding light rushed in followed by dark shadows screaming in Arabic. Hands grabbed my hair, as a rifle butt was pushed into my face, followed by torrents of kicks forcing me to scramble around in the dust. A powerful slap across my head numbed my senses and my reflexes automatically pulled my body into a foetal position, squirming in the dirt. I felt the reverberations around the building as the door banged shut and I was relieved to be left alone, again.

My adrenaline panic subsided. Slowly, I searched around and found a full water bottle and a paper bag containing a piece of chicken, some bread and dates. A sensation of happiness tingled through me as I wiped the blood from my nose. This bag contained the message of hope and a future. My captives wanted to keep me alive, but it was not until later, when I was squatting in

the corner listening to the movements and voices from
outside that I would wonder for how long.

Shake and Bake.

A flash of phosphorus white flew low across the night sky, followed by a dull thud and Fatima felt the vibration come up through the ground, her legs quivered. The dogs from the distant compound began to bark louder than she could recall and then after some sickening squeals, they were silent.

She and Hassan scrambled up the loose sandy incline and, lying prone, looked over the edge. They watched the dark outlines of the Paratroopers get up from their shallow scrapes. They were like creatures emerging from the earth with packs as encrusted shells on their backs, ands their faces blackened below the rounded silhouette of their helmets. They slowly converged towards the compound over which the flickering of flames, behind an orb of smoke, radiated a surreal faint glow from the huddle of burning buildings.

'Lets go,' Fatima said and tapped on Hassan's helmet. She got to her feet and stumbled on the loose gravel causing her camera bag to bounced hard against her hip. The unfamiliar weight of the flak jacket annoyed her and the hard leather from her helmet strap was rubbing under her chin.

The Israeli Media Ops insisted the Press wore protective clothing, they also insisted that reporters stay out of the fighting zone.

She and Hassan moved unnoticed, behind the military radio team, adding to the dark outlines of the troops crossing the ground into the compound.

She was after proof, to show the truth with photographs of the raw reality. Last week fifty civilians were treated for severe phosphorus burns in the Nasser hospital, amongst them was her youngest cousin Ahmid. The Israeli Defence Force, as always, had denied all responsibility.

'In here', Hassan whispered to Fatima. He grabbed her elbow and pulled her through a doorway into a small room. The flames lit up the compound and from the window they saw the burning remains of the dogs, and next to a smouldering woman a small child was wailing. Lumps of phosphorus were littered around pouring out white smoke. Across the yard they heard doors being smashed and felt the shudders from explosive bangs. Fatima's whole body was trembling as she clicked rapidly with her camera.

'Get the little girl,' she shouted at Hassan. He pushed another lump of phosphorus into his steel flask of water and closed the lid. He went out of the doorway, along the outside wall of the building, and lifted the young girl up onto his chest. She screamed, bit at his ear and pulled his hair trying to free herself.

'Shoo shoo, it's ok. You're ok,' he hushed her in Arabic, then ran back along the wall and met Fatima coming out of the doorway. They ran back towards the road to where their Toyota was parked, in a gully.

On the hotel television screen, the foreign secretary spokesman was speaking; "Yes, phosphorus was used but not in any illegal manner".

Fatima was watching but not listening to the spokesman. She held her mobile telephone to her ear and heard her mother repeat, 'Ahmid has just died.'

Treptower Park.

Her head was bowed and I came up to look into her face. We were alone on this cold February morning and the grey mist formed a layer of moisture over her hair. Her face, with its high cheeks, radiated a plain rustic beauty and her plaid was wrapped into a crown. The rumpled skin on her forehead defined her demure sadness.

In silence, I watched as tears flowed from under her eyes, they rolled down the side of her face to drip from beneath her chin. A few yards back, branches from the silver birch trees rustled the ground in a gentle breeze and the follicles on the back of my neck bristled. I was an intruder, and had been drawn in close by her posture, curious as to her discomfort.

I shuddered and realised that the representation of the tears was not an illusion. They were formed by the collection of the moisture on her head and channelled to her eye sockets by the furrows of her skin. The sculpture of Mother Russia was looking through me and I shivered in the ethereal sensation. I turned to view the reason for her mourning.

On either side of a fifty-meter wide, paved slope stood four rows of tall poplar trees. Each row was lined up in military precision as a representation of the ranks of the young men from Russia, whose bodies now massed in thousands beneath the ground. In front were smaller birch and willow trees, whose swaying branches rustled and skirted the ground, in depiction of the wives, daughters and girlfriends weeping over the graves.

I walked up the slope and could see at the top, on either side, two massive red marbled Soviet flags, lowered in honour to their fellow comrades. The incline was carefully designed so I was forced to lean forward and therefore lower my head in deserving respect for the dead, who had no influence in the decisions that had brought them here.

Two statues showing an old and a young soldier, their headdress removed, knelt by the front of each flag, as homage to the sacrifice of heroes. At the top of the slope between the flags was a large viewing veranda. Over the edge four symbolic graves were marked, a General, a Colonel, a Captain and a Soldier, apparently buried upright to form the review party of death's parade. The sight was immense and on either side more trees grew in precise rows and there were sixteen large sarcophagi positioned over the field, each with glorious battle carvings on the limestone. On one side the Cyrillic Russian and on the other the German describing the heroic symbolism of the Soviet power. The central view was of manicured lawn and hedges stretching over two hundred metres and almost as wide. Paths paved with polished mosaic stone lead to a grassy mould in the distance. Wide steps climbed up this conical form to a mausoleum on which stood a magnificent twelve-meter bronze statue of a Russian solider.

The soldier holds a child in his left arm and with an enormous sword in his right has smashed a swastika, which is stamped on by his left foot. His head is held high in arrogant defiance and he is looking east towards the centre of Berlin, the posture of the victorious holding the future of Germany in his arm.

The statue was inspired by the actions of Colour Sergeant Nikolai Masalov, the standard bearer of the 220th Guards Rifle Regiment. During a moment in the fighting, Sergeant Nikolai heard a child crying. He crossed a canal bridge and over open ground, whilst under fire from the German guns, ran to rescue the stunned infant sitting helpless next to the body of her dead mother. The child survived the war and grew up in an East Berlin orphanage. Sergeant Nikolai's body lies somewhere in this field beneath the roots of the poplar trees.

A plaque at my feet tells the story. The Soviet War Memorial, Treptower Park in Berlin, was designed by the architect Yakov Belapolsky and opened on 8th May 1945. The red marble, which forms the soviet flags, was taken from the ruins of the Reichstag building and the bronze statue of Sergeant Nikolai was cast in Leningrad.

The fine drizzle had stopped and a ray of sun pointed towards the city. I turned and walked along the wet pavement back to the S-Bahn. I was humbled by my thoughts of the horrific events and terrible destruction to which this memorial is a poignant reminder, but yet the sense of hope, embodied by the child in the soldier's arm, felt inspirational. I reflected on how politics seem detached from the reality of human destruction and death. Examples of hypocrisy remain today, which lay as a transparent cloth over the decisions that deal with such perceptions as calculating the balance between national pride and the value of lives.

I shifted the day sack on my back and I was overwhelmed by a weight of sadness.

Table by the Window.

Abigail sat at the table by the window, because she adored the view across the park. What a brilliant idea to have built her restaurant on this elevated spot, where, from within the dining room, all her guests could enjoy the vista of the open spaces while they ate. They would feel comfortable in the elegance of the interior décor, as they selected their gourmet meal, and still experience an ambience of the outdoors.

The park was full of the varieties of life, from the tiniest of insects, to birds on the lake, and a range of wild animals. It was also a place where leisurely people, walked their dogs, strolled for a breath of fresh air, or in colourful Lycra would jog along the wooded avenues. In the afternoons the restaurant veranda would be full of customers engaged in the pastime of people watching, while they consumed cream cakes with tea or coffee.

But Abigail's restaurant offered so much more than just coffee, and through the window she watched a young couple as they dawdled by, she smiled, if only they knew.

'Are you ready to eat, Miss?'

'Ah Preston, yes what's the soup today?'

'It's Wednesday, coriander and carrot Mistress, … sorry Miss.'

'Careful now, and the chicken, is it succulent and fresh?'

James McEwan

'Of course.' He grimaced, arranged her cutlery then turned and walked away. 'Of course, it is always fresh,' he said and shook his head.

She might have to get rid of Preston as he wasn't as astute these days and was, at times, insolent. He made mistakes, dangerous mistakes that might expose her past. She was the Mistress and Captain of culinary delights, but being called Mistress by Preston would turn her guests' attention towards her, and she would hear the whispered innuendos. They would then push their food around on their plates as if the green of the peas was some genetically modified discolouration. That won't do. She revelled in the thrill of watching her guests squirm with delight, when served with an elaborate presentation of food on their plate, and listen to them moan in ecstasy as they savoured the tastes of the dish. Perfection. It was a discourtesy to allow Preston's behaviour to distract them from their food.

'Your soup Miss.'

'This is mushroom and dandelion. But that's our Friday menu Preston.'

'Yes, today is Friday.'

'Are all the ingredients fresh?'

'Early this morning Miss, baby Liberty Caps direct from the park.' He grinned and walked away. 'Of course, magic mushrooms and sweet dreams.'

Abigail was a Gothic princess and, on the opening night, she flaunted her status by wearing; a dark velvet cape, laced boots, her ceremonial knives and titanium jewellery, which were the symbols of her royal patronage. However, it was a costume that attracted some curious and weird voyeurs. She had also forced Preston to wear his gossamer body suit that was made from the skin of his dead, pet python. The fool, he over did his role with his hissed and clipped way of speaking. A pubescent girl had sat terrified by his manner of preceding every sentence with a slow "Yesss Mistresss", and he had a wriggling rat's tail hung from his mouth. The traumatised girl ran out with urine trickling down her legs, unforgettable and unforgivable.

The evening was a disaster. These people were not ready for Abigail's sophisticated style, and this unfortunate start dissuaded the true gourmet diners. There had to be change.

Over night, she had revamped the restaurant and changed her clothes for a light business suit. It made her feel almost human. She chose a light-grey theme with maroon bow ties for the staff uniforms and ordered them to carry brilliant white napkins. However, it was typical of Preston to object and he refused to tuck in his shirt, until she threatened to send him home.

When it came to foraging for food, Preston was her expert and so it was inconceivable she would send him away. For instance, he was an expert on identifying wild mushrooms and herbs, and he knew how to hunt the deer. There were also other creatures that roamed the park at night, and Preston always had this speciality meat ready and hung in the cooler for the next evening's dinner. Abigail's adventurous menu offered fox, badger, rabbit and the oily eels from the lake. These were disguised as chicken and lamb that was served in a rustic curry or soup. Preston could always be trusted to be discrete, particularly as to the source of the "reality meat" for the cottage pies served on theme nights.

Her favourite guests were from the county courts, the lawyers and their staff, who demanded cannibal evenings, "for just a bit of fun". An inebriated secretary once remark, on how life like the stuffed heads of the children looked, centrally plated as décor on the table. Preston, the idiot, had taken a liberty and had left their eyes intact.

'Your coriander and carrot soup, Miss'

'But I've just had mushroom, where has the plate gone?'

'That was Friday, it's Wednesday Miss.'

She must not be misled by Preston's inept attempt to distort time, elusive as he may be. But shock does that to you, it pins you to the spot with a crystallised picture of the moment, and your mind fractures beyond repair. It has taken him two days to bring soup from the kitchen, yes that has to be the reason. Her last black out was over a month ago, and she had recovered. So why is Preston lying?

Outside the window is where real life begins. For instance, the same man arrives and sits on a bench, always at one, just before she is served her soup. He wears a different shirt every day, and is always writing, or sketching or maybe he doodles in that notepad he holds on his lap.

'Preston, will you please invite that man to join me?'

'No Miss, he might be a policeman.'

'Tell him we are having champagne.'

'No Miss, what about the twins?'

Will Preston ever forget, everyone else has. The twins had gone missing after their picnic in the park, but it was not their fault. That day, Preston had rushed out on request from a wealthy diner, meat for a plate that had to be filled. The police had come searching the restaurant like hounds sniffing for truffles, but failed to find the missing children.

'Make it pink champagne. Would he resist licking and lapping as it trickles over me? Would he linger with his tongue if a pool collects in my navel?'

Oh, the days when the park was a royal hunting ground where her entourage of princes could enjoy their afternoon of blood sport, and at night gorge on the meat of venison and pheasants. They would drink wine late into the night and ravage the maidens, who they had found wandering in the woods, as punishment for trespassing on her Gothic land. That was her world, but something had gone wrong, where time had been distorted by a few hundred years.

'Yes Miss.' Preston stomped off. 'Of course pink champagne, it is always pink.'

She looked back to the bench but the man had gone. Her soup tasted of insects and oily fish.

That evening she showed them to their table, the session of the court, as she liked to call them, they were all eager for their mock cannibal feast. The man from the park bench was also there. In fact, he was the centre of attention for those who sat around the table, because his eyes stared out at them from his handsome head displayed on a sliver tray. The secretaries screamed and the lawyers shouted obscenities. They said the poor man's name was Joseph, who wouldn't have eaten a fly.

'Preston, you idiot.'

'You boast authentic meals for the demanding diner.' Preston sneered.

'I hate you Preston.' She will have to leave this dimension now. What a pity, it was such a beautiful park and a great place in time.

The restaurant in the park disappeared overnight and buried on the residual mound was a mixture of bones, both animal and human remains. A detailed forensics examination confirmed, through dental records, that the children's sculls they found were those of the missing twins, Abigail and Preston Fletcher.

Snow White.

Last night I dreamed of the dark forests and of the seven rugged mountains that encircled our hidden land. In my nightmare, the old witch in the market place had gripped my hand and ran her sharp black nails across my palm to draw out crimson lines of blood.

'You have the heart of a prince,' she screeched, 'you are the one. You must find her. Go to the forest and find the lost child.' She flapped her arms in the air. 'The child will save us all.' A gust of wind blew down from the turrets of the castle and engulfed her in a cloud of swarming flies that tore her into rags and dust.

The villagers stood silent, staring, as they were defeated men and women who were tired of resistance and their drudgery of life. I dreamed of monsters, dragons and creatures, that sucked the blood from men and horses, they would swoop at night and devour anyone who moved. My feverish nightmares lasted for seven weeks, and in my apparitions I fought with wolves and women, who screamed as they transformed into hideous beasts that bit the heads from newborn babies.

Then the dreams stopped. I felt fresh and strong, and no longer afraid of the darkness or the demigods that roamed in the forest.

'What does all this mean?' I pointed at my trusted friend Black Cap.

'It's the work of the Queen. She has cursed our land with fear and allows the demons to roam at night. Once the rivers flowed with fresh water and the fields were full of fruit and corn, but now they are dry and the standing water is foul and so bitter, whatever crop does grow, it is pitiful.'

I knew the queen was hated, but to learn that she was the cause of our miserable existence and the reason of my dreams, I became infuriated and felt the blood pumping in my veins.

'Can't you see how all the women are wrinkled and old and their husbands prefer to sleep in the shed amongst their pigs.' Black Cap continued his story in a whisper as if I had opened a forbidden book. We huddled in the alcove by the ruinous church where the wilted roses hung gasping for water. Black Cap pulled his woollen cape around him and held his jewelled handled sword close to his chest, he stroked thoughtfully at his long chin with its his van dyke beard, and beads of perspirations dropped from his hooked nose.

'The Queen was Princess Cleopatra from the black moon and she came to this land to form a marriage of alliance with the King. When she discovered he already had a wife and daughter, she sent an army of demons to destroy the land. The King and Queen along with the baby princess were taken deep into the forest and murdered by Cleopatra's huntsman.' Tears rolled down Black Cap's cheeks as he spoke. 'Rumours from the woodsmen now roam the market places. They say the baby Princess is still alive and has grown into a beautiful angel. The villagers secretly pray to this angel, who they call Snow White. Should she return, they believe the magical powers of Queen Cleopatra would fail, and the country would once again be free and prosperous.'

'Then we must find Snow White.' I stood up and drew my sword, pointing it defiantly into the air, I said, 'let's find her and set the people free.'

The breeze tussled my hair and my cape fluttered and flapped, sounding like loud applause.

'These are just rumours, tales of foolish women around the market places.'

'Yes, but what if they are true. We must rescue the beautiful Snow White from the dark forest. Are you with me Black Cap?'

That evening, when the moons of the white, the yellow and the black aligned as one in the sky and so the night was at its darkest, we set off. Black Cap and I followed along the mountainous trails, walking with our horses until the moons separated, and in the dim light we found the overgrown route out of our hidden land.

We travelled through the night and when the morning glow rose over the peaks of the mountains, we reached a clearing with a small hamlet. There were three buildings; one a thatched straw cottage, another made of wood and on a small hillock stood a strong brick house.

'Well then handsome visitors,' said a sweet female voice, 'you are early today.'

I turned and saw the young woman standing by the straw house door. She curtsied and smiled. Her white face contrasted with the black of her hair, and her lacy dress was drawn tight about her waist.

'Are you Snow White?' Demanded Black Cap.

'Oh, you are a grumpy one.' She tilted her head and looked us up and down. Her eyes sparkled. 'Why don't you get off your horses and come in for some tea. You must be hungry. I am.' She licked her lips and said, 'yes, I am so hungry.'

I dismounted from my horse and stretched my legs.

A second young woman appeared in the doorway of the wooden house and came to join us. 'What is it Glynis? Who are these people?'

'This is Gwen?' Glynis said and pointed at us. 'They are looking for Snow White.'

'Gwenyth,' shouted Gwen and looked up towards the brick house. Gwenyth came running down the hillock towards us. Her fresh milky complexion shimmered in the sunshine, and her black hair trailed in the wind as she ran.

Black Cap remained on his horse, it snorted and stamped around the clearing. I followed the young ladies into the straw house. When I entered through the door a large black wolf leapt past me and landed in the room. The women turned towards it and their bodies transformed into hideous vampires, who snarled at the growling werewolf. They leapt onto its back and they tore and bit into the fur. The wolf shook the vampires off and snapped with its powerful jaws into the necks of the hideous creatures, it spat out blood and drool. As each woman fell, their bodies gently metamorphosed into piglets that squirmed and twitched towards death. The werewolf turned and pinned me to the ground, its snarling teeth inches from my eyes, and dripped blood onto my face. Lifting its head it gave a blood-curling howl and then ran out of the door.

I stumbled back out of the cottage to where Black Cap was waiting with my horse. We rode at a fast gallop further into the forest, through and between the trees, letting the horses find the way.

We stopped for a rest and sat by a trickling stream.

'Now you understand why the men are drawn to sleep with their pigs.' Black cap muttered and chuckled.

'Never mind that. How I am to recognise the real Snow White?'

'They say she has a birth mark that looks like a tiny tear drop behind her left ear.'

After resting we followed the stream up the valley to a large dam. The lake behind it stretched far away towards the horizon.

'Ah, this is why the land is so parched.' I said and realised now that Cleopatra's influence stretched far into the forests and beyond our hidden land. A rhythmic sound of singing began and became louder, moving towards us. "Hi zumba zumba zay, hi zumba zumba zay..."

We hid amongst a thicket of bushes and watched as a group of dwarfs, workmen from the dam, marched past in time to their incantations. Out of sight, we followed them to a forest cottage and observed them from behind a small hillock as they hung up their tools. Through an open window we saw them sat at a table, eating and laughing. In through one of the side windows we saw a young woman, who had a smooth round face, and she was combing her long black hair.

I looked at Black Cap, who smiled at me, and he tugged at his beard. He nodded.

We rushed down to the cottage, knocked at the door, and when there was no immediate reply, we went straight in. All the heads of the small workmen turned to us, their eyes were bloodshot and their faces the colour of grey ash, on the table was the fresh corpse of what was once a woodsman. They leapt up screaming with blood dripping from their mouths, it was as if dessert had arrived and each wanted the sweetest part.

'Stop it,' shouted the young woman, who had stuck her head through the kitchen hatch. The zombie midgets transformed back into happy smiling dwarfs and tucked into what was left of the woodsman on the table. I had drawn my sword and dagger and moved precariously to the hatch. The girl smiled and I had a flashback to

Glynis' cheeky grin. I put the dagger point to her nose, she turned away and then I saw the tear drop mark below her left ear.

'Snow White?' I said.

The dwarfs stopped eating, they turned towards us and watched.

'And you are?' she said, 'another of Cleopatra's huntsmen?'

The dwarfs stood up holding pieces of meat dripping with blood.

'No. I've come to take you back home.' I noticed that Black Cap had left the room.

The dwarfs sat down unperturbed and resumed their feast.

I looked through the hatch and saw how her body was formed into a large bulbous blob on which her head appeared as small nodule.

'This is Cleopatra's spell, "If you want to be Queen", she had said, "then you are Queen Bee", not funny eh.' Snow White's eyes welled up and she blew her nose with a lace handkerchief.

The dwarfs all burst out laughing and repeated, 'Queen Bee, Hi zumba zumba zay, Queen Bee.'

'You better go,' Snow White said, 'don't stay the night because tomorrow you will be their breakfast.'

The door burst open and a werewolf leapt in onto the table; it tore the head off a dwarf and started to attack the rest. I joined in and decapitate two of them and stabbed my dagger through the eye of another. Blood splashed up the walls and all the dying bodies flapped like landed fish as they metamorphosed into dwarf piglets. The wolf spat out some fingers, lifted its head and howled before running out of the door.

Through the hatch I saw that Snow White had fainted. I kicked in the locked kitchen door and lifted her small head onto my lap. She was so beautiful despite the hideous body. I brushed aside some of her hair and impulsively kissed her birthmark.

A loud, snarling growl made me turn and there in the door way stood the werewolf, ready to pounce. It leapt forward with a great roar; instinctively I stabbed my sword into its body and drove my dagger deep into its chest. The wolf dropped at my feet squirming. Its canine body changed form to reveal Black Cap. I knelt beside him and lifted his head.

'What have I done?' I gasped.

'You have done right,' Black Cap spluttered, 'I was sent to kill Snow White.'

'Why?'

'I was the huntsman who killed Snow White's family. I couldn't kill a small child. When Cleopatra found out she cursed me with this werewolf spell.' He spluttered blood and it sprayed over his chin and beard. 'She promised to retract the curse when Snow White was finally dead.'

He started to laugh and he reached up to lock my neck in a deadly choking grip.

'Ha,' he screamed, ' you can't kill me, you fool.'

A sharp wooden splinter from the door was rammed from behind, deep into Black Cap's chest, and he released his grip on my throat. Snow White pushed it deeper into his body. Black Cap metamorphosed into a dead black boar. My kiss had released Snow White from her bulbous form back into a beautiful young princess.

She hugged me.

On the way back home we released the dam and let the water flow out of the mountains into our land.

We never saw Cleopatra again, but heard from the villagers of the story about a large sow being chased from the castle through the market. The fresh water

James McEwan

flowed into the valley and restored the beauty of the
women; all the pigs in the land were given anti-vampire
serum and were cured. The men slept once again with
their wives, and babies no longer had their heads bitten
off in the night.

Snow White became the true Queen of our land.
Although we were not married, I was rewarded with the
knowledge that our land was now free, prosperous and
full of honey.

It was rumoured in the marketplaces that Snow
White was clearly happy, because everyone could hear
her singing as she buzzed like a bee around the castle.

Torn Sisters.

Aileen slipped the letter back into the envelope that was addressed in a familiar scrawl. One by one she flicked away the blossom that landed on her knees. Holding a wine glass pressed against her bottom lip she leaned back and turned her face towards the morning sun. Her husband, Cameron, had been the talkative type and you wouldn't imagine he had a secret. Her instincts were right. If only he had said something. It was his writing on the envelope, "Personal for Mary Chapman".

She sipped the wine, savouring its almond flavour, and watched a butterfly flutter over the table. The blue spots on its wings shifted like inquisitive eyes as it came closer. Aileen remained motionless. What should she do? Mary has to go. The butterfly hovered, settled and sucked at the fluid from the inside of the bottle's neck.

How ironic to share Cameron's last Chateau d'Yquem with a beautiful peacock butterfly. If only it was true as he had said, that when we died our souls were reincarnated. We'd all be free like butterflies to flitter over the hedgerows and search for nectar amongst the flowers and wild roses.

Aileen closed her eyes. In her mind she had hold of Cameron's hand on their honeymoon by the Dordogne. The warm wind had tussled her hair and blown magnolia petals around her like confetti. He had laughed and waving them away stopped to kiss her.

'I love you, Mary,' he had whispered. He didn't realise what he'd said, and how unforgivable to think of Mary. Then he cried, 'Oh no, no, no, sorry … Aileen.'

She had made him kneel in a grovelling apology, his face paled, his eyes watered, he begged for forgiveness.

'Promise Cameron, promise or it ends now,' she had screamed at him.

A woman shouted from the top of the garden. 'Hello. There you are.'

Aileen sat forward and the butterfly took off. She looked up towards the house and with her hand shielded her eyes from the sun. She saw it was Mary.

'I was knocking at the front door,' Mary called out. She laughed as she came down the path with a basket and a flat parcel gripped under her arm. Her rugby top was faded and the light cotton trousers stained with coloured paint. A ponytail tied loosely failed to contain some wild strands of her black hair. 'What a fantastic morning,' she said, 'doesn't it feel good to be alive?'

'So you came,' Aileen said. She drained her glass and refilled it. Mary's cheerfulness was annoying. She watched as her sister pushed the basket across the garden table and slumped onto a wooden chair. Mary picked up a bottle and checked the label; she swiped away the blossom on her shoulders and stared at Aileen.

'So what! It's a beautiful day and lovely wine.' Aileen sipped from her glass.

'It's only eleven in the morning and . . . ' Mary stopped when Aileen lifted the white envelope in the air. 'Ah the letter, are you sure that's Cameron's writing?'

'Don't you know?' Aileen threw it across the table. 'Off course it's his and you know damn well. So give me your version.'

Mary put the envelope under the basket. 'It's probably just the cheque for the portrait.'

'Open it.' Aileen shouted. 'Tell me. I want to hear what you have to say.'

Cameron had bought paintings from Mary, dark awful impressionist landscapes. It was a shock to have found them hidden behind the coal in the cellar with the price tags still attached. With little notes, lots of hand written intimate notes, "Thank you, love Mary", and a date. Behind them was the box from France marked, "White for Aileen, Red for Mary". On top was the envelope. So much for the promise by the Dordogne and so much for three years of happiness to be shattered like crystal glass. How could Cameron have been so stupid?

'Oh Aileen really, it's just a cheque for the portrait … I'll open it later. How about a glass of wine first?'

'He left you the Pemorol.' Aileen pointed at the bottles of red on the table.

'Look I've brought lunch.' Mary started to unpack. There were sandwiches and a large chocolate cake. 'Are you hungry? Ham and tomato was Cameron's favourite with this red.'

'No they weren't, he liked smoked salmon and white.'

Mary stopped for a moment. 'Well, yes, … you'd know wouldn't you.'

'Sod you. I'll get a glass and some plates.'

Aileen walked across the lawn to the house. Mary had said she was bringing a portrait and it was thoughtful of her to bring the picnic. Fresh sandwiches were just what she needed to soak up the wine, almost half the bottle already. Cornflakes on top of last night's feast of strawberries came straight back up this morning and the sight of Mary's chocolate cake was enough to start hunger rumbles in anyone's stomach.

Cameron had never mentioned buying Mary's paintings and such monstrosities. His interest in fine art like the James Patrick paintings that hung in the hall made sense. Mary's crap on the other hand should be burnt on the bonfire. What was he thinking?

She lifted some plates and a glass from the dishwasher. She gave them a quick rinse and a wipe, and then she slipped a kitchen knife under her waistband.

Back in the garden Mary was grinning as she took the glass and plates from Aileen. The sandwiches were spread on a foil tray together with some small pancakes and buttered scones. The cake had been sliced.

'What do you think?' She pointed to the portrait standing against the apple tree.

Aileen sat down with a sandwich and her glass of wine. She stared. In the painting Cameron was reclined in front of the willow trees by the river. He was magnificent. This was where he had proposed to her, kneeling and squinting with the sun in his face. At the time, the raspberries had melted in her mouth bursting the bubbles of the pink champagne and the diamond had sparkled on the ring. This was their place forever. Where solitude and togetherness merged in her memories of those lazy afternoons with the warmth of the summer sun. In the foreground of the painting were his favourite butterflies above the forget-me-nots and clover. He looked much younger and the vivid colours with the smooth texture of his features were so life like. It must have taken months to paint, and with such precision, and in such intimate detail.

Mary stood as if a statue, smiling and staring at the painting. She held her glass to her lips. The fresh fruity flavours of the wine conjured images of her in Cameron's arms by the river. It was their place, always. At the time, she had been sketching the willow tree, with its yellow catkins, where the branches skirted the water. Cameron had appeared floundering out from the sweet-grass and bulrush reeds, where he was stalking after butterflies or so he had said. How could anyone not giggle? He was chopping in the muddy waters and had swiped away at the insects above his head.

His hand had felt firm and tight as she helped him onto the solid ground where she tripped him. He'd struggled as they rolled on the grass, but gave up in a fit of laughter. He compared her sketches to the art of Leonardo de Vinci and then he asked, no he had demand her, to do his portrait.

It was a long summer and every day painting with slow brush strokes by the river was bliss.

Mary had later qualified for a place at the London Art College and Cameron came up every weekend from Salisbury. He had bought carnations in Waterloo station to inspire her, and he called her his starving artist. They ate Dim Sum with rice in Gerrard Street and gorged on lasagne in Covent Garden. At night in the attic room, filled with the aroma of the percolated coffee from the café below, they huddled naked in the winter under layers of duvets.

It was bitter cold that night when he telephoned, his garbled voice buzzed as if wasps had nested in her mind. It was over. Afterwards, the London flat became an empty lonely place. She hung the painting above the old Victorian fireplace and for company she would read to it, the painting of Cameron smiling by the river.

Then she had a baby. With baby Lewis she couldn't afford the fun of city life and after two years of squalor had no choice. She came home, back to Salisbury where the willows by the river still grew, just as she had painted them in the portrait.

Mary drunk back her wine and refilled the glass.

'Mary, it is so realistic and so alive,' Aileen said, 'I wasn't expecting this.'

'Alive! Maybe in spirit but quite dead.'

'Mary!' Aileen turned to her sister. 'How depressing … it was an accident.'

'Yes of course … it was an accident.' Mary reached for more wine. 'Like as if Cameron would fall off cliffs everyday.'

Aileen bit on her bottom lip. The smile in the portrait seemed to move and implored her to stretch over and touch him.

Mary pointed at the portrait. 'Don't you think baby Lewis has Cameron's eyes?'

'No! Not really, where is he anyway?' Aileen reached for another sandwich.

'I've left him with Granny.' Mary refilled her glass. 'He calls Sophie, "Granny".'

'Sophie is not his grandmother. You know you shouldn't be so encouraging.'

'He's only two, still a baby.' Mary shooed away the butterflies around the wine bottle. 'For goodness sake.'

'I don't mean your Lewis,' Aileen snapped. 'I mean Sophie, Cameron's mother, and you know damn well.'

'What's the harm, she loves him.' Mary wiped cake crumbs from her lips.

'Dad called you a promiscuous tart when he heard about the baby.' Aileen smirked. 'Why didn't you marry the father?'

'I couldn't.' Mary slumped in her chair. 'He was married.'

Aileen shook her head. 'Dad was so disappointed with you. He said Mum was spared the shame. But really, I'm sure she would have been delighted.'

'I could have married.' Mary filled her glass. 'If he wasn't so damn spineless.'

'I'm not interested in your London affairs. Now open the envelope and read it out.'

'It's sad, what happened to Cameron, as you said he was so alive.' Mary licked the chocolate from her fingers and drained her glass of wine. 'No Aileen, I won't open the envelope it's private.' She wasn't going to read this out in front of Aileen. 'I don't know how to tell you, except to say, Cameron is Lewis's father.'

'Mary, bugger off. You don't know, it's the wine talking.'

'I've proof, Cameron's been paying for years.'

'You've been blackmailing him, you bastard.'

'Technically he has been buying my paintings.' Mary laughed.

'Well that's the end of it.' Aileen stood up. 'Read the letter and go back to London.'

She went to the portrait and threw the wine from her glass over Cameron and pulled out the knife from her waistband. Mary watched, poured herself another wine and brushed away the dead butterflies from the table.

'I will move into this house. Cameron's beautiful house, Lewis's house.' Mary said and drank more wine. 'You'll have to sell, you've no choice.'

Aileen dropped to her knees. It seemed she was grovelling as Cameron had done in the Dordogne. The portrait seemed alive as if mocking her with a constant smile from under the willows. This was never their place. It was Mary's and his. She reached out and touched Cameron's face on the painting. He had knelt on the hard stones in the Dordogne and held her hand like a pleading child. His promise was based on fear instead of honesty and truth. It was not forgiveness she wanted but an understanding of why he didn't tell her. Was he so afraid of her passionate threats as the magnolia petals had scattered and scurried away along the path?

She drove the knife into the portrait and slashed the canvas from the face to its body. Years of its silent whisperings of hope for Mary were torn apart. Over.

'This is the end of it Mary … It stops now.' Aileen screamed and turned.

'Cameron!' Mary shouted. 'Aileen, you bastard.' She leapt forward with the cake knife and slashed at Aileen. Missed. Aileen knocked it from Mary's hand and tripped her over onto the grass. She grabbed the ponytail, pushed her knee into her back and pulled to expose Mary's neck.

'Please Aileen …Please don't.' Mary started to retch and splutter over the grass.

'Do you realise what you've done.' Aileen held the knife against her throat.

'Me! No it was you.' Mary twisted her body and retched. 'You've poisoned me, you bitch.' She gurgled in her vomit.

'It's over, it all ends now.'

'Aileen, please.' Mary went limp. 'Lewis. … What about Lewis.' She spluttered and her body convulsed in spasmodic jerks, she was gasping for air.

Aileen let her go, stood up and threw the knife away. 'Get up you stupid bitch.' She grabbed Mary under the arms and helped her onto a chair.

'Lean forward, keep your head down,' she told Mary. 'I'll get a doctor.'

Mary was unconscious when the ambulance arrived.

'No I don't want to come.' Aileen told the medics and poured herself another wine.

The flames at the bottom of the garden flashed bright colours from the chemicals in the burning paint. Aileen threw another dark landscape onto the fire.

'Aileen.' A woman shouted from the top of the garden. 'I've been knocking for ages.' Sophie in a white blouse and flora-patterned skirt strode across the lawn. She gave Aileen a long firm hug.

'Should you be doing this?' Sophie swung her hands in the air. 'Look at all this smoke.'

'I'm fine, don't worry.' Aileen threw the scene of the willows onto the hot ashes and watched Cameron's image melt in the heat.

'That's the last one. Its over now,' she said. Aileen poked at the fire with a long stick.

The stick reminded her of DI Dobson's fat finger that had poked her forehead. Most attempted murders are domestic he prodded. The analysts found methanol in the red wine but forensics tests could not establish evidence of tampering. Dobson kept mumbling, he wasn't convinced after he examined Cameron's letter.

"Mary,

I have sent a copy of this medical report to my solicitor for future reference. Here's your copy. The DNA results show that I am not Lewis's father. Now I want you out of my life."

'Mary has gone back to London,' Sophie said. 'Shame I'll miss little Lewis.'

'Perhaps when she finds his father,' Aileen said, 'they'll come to visit one day.' Aileen smiled, perhaps and more likely they won't after what'd happened. 'Mary just needs some time.'

Sophie patted Aileen's belly. 'Well are you going to tell. Is it a boy or a girl?'

'It's far too early, let's just wait and see.' Aileen smiled.

Muscles John.

It was the light that woke him but it was terror that kept him awake. The beam, from headlights on the road, shone directly through the thin curtains and filled his bedroom with shadows, and dark grotesque shapes that chased each other along the walls and leapt as if to escape an unseen menace. These twisted images intensified Allan's erratic thoughts, balancing illogically on a knife-edge that denied him the sleep he craved.

Overwhelmed by worry about the consequence of his decision that had invoked the threats from Muscles John, he lay each night in a paralysis and afraid to sleep. Whenever he dozed into the warmth and safety of his pillows the light beams sent shadows around him, he could only retreat beneath the sheets to hide from their mockery. What had he agreed to do?

'You don't want to know what'll happen if this goes wrong,' Muscles John had said, 'I'll see you on Saturday then.' With his calloused hands he had grabbed Allan by the collars of his jacket and shook him. 'Now, don't be late.'

'No Allan.' His friends and Iain had warned him. 'Stay away, it will be like a death sentence and you'll be chained to the debt with no escape.'

'You'll regret it. It's not worth it.' Iain had told him. 'Think about your freedom and what you'll be giving up.'

He only wanted to make a change in his life, to give up slogging along the streets every day delivering letters. His vision for the future and his dream, with his girlfriend Julia, was to own a restaurant and Muscles John had suggested a solution, but there were conditions.

Admiration, that's it, he should admire Muscles John despite the backslapping and uncomfortably tight hugs. He was not sure how to respond to the hard headed and hot-tempered John from the old school of common sense, he just smiled and agreed to everything in his presence. How could he not admire him? The man started as a boy dealing in scrap iron from the dismantling of the railways and had used his gains over the years to build a large property portfolio. When two associates disappeared after attempting to defraud him on a multilevel car park deal, it was reputed that John had buried them on his golf course. Allen wished he hadn't asked him about the Jolly Roger at the thirteenth hole, John had just winked and gave a wide menacing grin.

He felt his stomach tighten and pulled the pillow beneath the sheets, it'll be all right, won't it?

On Saturday morning, Allan stood shaving while he confronted a picture of Muscles John he kept above the sink. 'You don't scare me.' Allan took a deep breath to steady his hand as he carefully run the blade over his face. He didn't want any blood on his collar, not today of all days. Iain had said he would bring a gun.

'No guns,' Allan had said.

Allan and Iain met on time and waited for Muscles John to arrive. Allan kept stroking his face. It was important to have a clean shave and he shifted from one foot to the other.

'Don't worry. I've got it with me.' Iain gave him an anxious smile. He patted his jacket pocket.

Allan's legs trembled and almost buckled beneath him when he heard the door of the hall open. In walked Muscles John dressed in his Oxford Row suit, his large head beaming with that intimidating smile. A girl's soft hand rested on his wrist, a hush followed by a moment's silence within the hall as everyone turned and they saw Julia in her gown. She was beautiful and the organ music played while Muscles John walked his daughter down the aisle.

The List.

My dear wife Ruth loved me, I know because she ended every sentence obsessively with the words, "love you". This was a subconscious reflex on her part and destroyed my attempts to win any domestic debate or even argue sensibly. How could I? She would nip the air with "I don't think so, love you". Subconsciously my mind would respond, "hate you", an endless repetitive dictum which over decades developed my fantasy of plotting her demise.

Our married life was ruled by a precision of lists and specific order of events, jobs to be done, programmes or films to watch, books to read and friends to call. I did agree that birthdays and anniversary listed on the calendar made sense. However, she was oblivious to the standing jokes by her colleagues in the library or even the obvious mimicking from the milkman, "I'll add whipped cream to the list Mrs Cornice, love you".

But the Saturday shopping list was the nightmare of them all, a different list for each Saturday of the month to be repeated every four weeks. Washing powder on the first Saturday, cooking oil second Saturdays only, and so it went on. The meticulously planned route through the supermarket would ensure all the items were collected in the correct order. Every item was placed into the trolley and subsequently removed to ensure the receipt provided proof of correctness and corresponded line for line on the list. Ruth was distraught when our local Tesco shop reorganised the layout of the aisles. She had to tell the manager it was unthinkable, love you.

Today I was ecstatic, in the supermarket I didn't have a list and my route was as random as bee in search of pollen. I ignored the sliced bread normally on every list. I avoided the fish counter, a third Saturday item. I collected a bottle of German red Dornfelder wine - never on any list. I thought, if only she knew what I was planning today, a large cut of Italian ham, succulent moist and delicious on crusty French bread. A sweet mango and a pineapple, items I would normally pass by to collect the oranges on her list. Toiletries were on Wednesday's list, the only day she would shop alone and I was occasionally treated to the same old bar of shaving cream.

But today, well, I added shaving gel and a new Gillette open razor because yesterday, I had sharpened and used my old razor for the last time.

I loved my dear wife, but her obsession for lists and ritual precision certainly lead to my unbearable frustration, no children and psychopathic madness. However, I know she was absolutely right, and that premeditated thought with perfect plans noted on a chronological list would ensure that every eventuality was considered. Her intelligent application of idealism, order and doctrine of neatness could never be faulted, and that is why I know; no one will ever miss my dear obsessive wife or ever discover where she has gone.

Torture.

I was late, and rushed along the pavement dodging past the meandering pedestrians when a woman stopped suddenly in front of me. I quickly sidestepped, knocking my elbow on a lamppost and spilled my Costa coffee all down my woollen trousers. The woman's German Shepard leapt at me. To avoid its dirty paws I skipped backwards onto the road and was hit by a car, and catapulted upwards. In the moment it took me to rattle over the bonnet I saw the passenger. She instinctively flinched and grabbed at the driver. Her red hair was hanging out from beneath a woollen beanie, and her eyes focused on mine as I bounced off the windscreen. I saw my world turning in a peripheral blur.

I felt a euphoria wash over me, as if floating in a tropical sea, it was warm and I saw strands of seaweed rhythmically wave about me like soft hair blowing in a gentle wind. I was comfortable but couldn't move, and feeling as if stuck in mud, and from behind my eyelids I sensed a bright light shining on my face. I heard a door bang, I opened my eyes to a conscious realisation and moaned when I saw where I was.

'Mr Lefontain, you are with us today,' the nurse said, leaning over me so I could see her face. 'The doctor will be along soon and he'll explain what's happened.' She then started to fill out the form on a clipboard, taking readings from the array of machines I was attached to. 'Now don't worry, you'll be fine.' She adjusted a valve on one of the tubes connected into the back of my hand and my mind began to bob once more like floating on the waves of a sea. My mouth was dry and tasted of almonds with their subtle smell lingering in my nostrils. I wanted to reach down and scratch at my legs to free them from the itching and the mud, I couldn't understand why I was stuck in mud or drifting like flotsam on the sea.

The door banged again and a group of people surrounded my bed like great white sharks preparing to devour the remains of a dying whale. I smelt the old spice aftershave preceding the appearance of a man's unshaved face looking down over me.

'I'm Doctor Schneider. Don't worry everything is fine,' he said and started to fiddle with the machines. 'You have broken legs. They are mending fine. The nurse will remove the collar from your neck. There is no external damage to your head. You will soon be able to sit up. How is that?' He didn't wait for a reply but turned and walked away followed by his shoal in white coats.

Later that day, I managed to sit up when a young policewoman came to tell me about the white Mercedes that had hit me. The driver did not stop. A pedestrian got the registration, JPO 507C; nevertheless the vehicle and its owner were still missing and unidentified.

At this news, I shuffled uncomfortably on the bed and the itch beneath the plaster cast on my legs intensified. I asked where my backpack with its laptop and my mobile was, but she didn't know. However, she made a note of their disappearance and will search for them as part of her investigation. I had been identified from the business card in my wallet, she told me, as Mr John Lefontain from 28 Lamb Street London. My work colleagues had been very helpful. She reassured me that the culprit would be found. I smiled and attempted a little wave as she left.

I picked up one of the get-well cards from the side table and stared at the name, I knew who owned the Mercedes and decided the police didn't need to know, not yet anyway.

Drifting between sleep and boredom I was glad this time to hear the door bang. Iain had arrived alone.

'Hi Iain, thanks for coming,' I said and moved around on my elbows adjusting myself upwards on the bed, Iain helped by placing a pillow behind me.

'Whoa, you look awful,' he said and smiled. 'Have you broken both your legs? Cool.'

'How's everyone at the shop?' I ignored his insensitivity.

'All Ok, the new autumn range has come in and it is selling well.'

'That's one of the new jackets you are wearing, isn't it?'

'Yes, this one with the Black Watch pattern is selling great.' He opened up the buttons to show me the label and I saw his dark glasses stuck into the pen pocket.

'It was the Mercedes that ran me over,' I said, 'the one we used for the photo shoots.'

He ignored me and poured himself a glass of water, and sat down on a chair before he took a long gulp.

'Its not roadworthy, you're kidding yourself,' he said, his smile had gone. 'Look it can't be the Mercedes. You must be confused, you've had a bang on your head.'

'Its not registered or insured, that's why the police can't find its owner.'

He got up and turning his back on me went to look out of the window.

'Was it you driving the car Iain?'

'Did you see the driver?' He spoke, while watching a flock of starlings fly past the window.

'No. But I saw Laura and she never goes anywhere without you,' I shouted at him.

The room door opened and Laura came to the foot of my bed, there were tears flooding down her face. Now I knew for certain, who it was in the car, but all I could do was stare at Laura. She looked tired with puffed rings beneath her eyes, her long red hair rested on her shoulders contrasting against the white of her Arran sweater, and that woollen beanie was still stuck on her head. They were wearing the same clothes they had on a few days ago and I wondered why no one had described their attire to the police.

'We are really sorry,' she said, looking down at her feet. 'You are not going to tell the police, are you?' She lifted her head and looked directly into my eyes.

Aghast, I saw the same scared expression replicated in my mind. It was the face I saw when I bounced across the car's windscreen. I held her stare, wondering to myself about the real meaning of friendship.

'You don't want Iain to go to prison do you?' She said. 'John. Please, he is your best friend.' She clasped her hands and unclasped her hands then looked across at Iain.

No he is not, he is just a work colleague and yes, Ok he is a friend and, a partner in the business. But running me over in my own car? What, was I to think.

The Mercedes SL Class Roadster was my grandfather's dream when he bought it in 1965. He left it to me and since then I have had the seats restored with the original tan leather. I spent hours on the body and even resourced the original paint colour from the factory in Bavaria, to retain the original classic sheen.

'Where is the car, is there much damage?' I snapped. If only I could reach that irritation, that constant itching under the cast on my legs.

'I put it back in your mother's garage,' Iain spoke quietly, 'nothing you can't fix.' He took hold of Laura's hand. 'I am sorry John…'

'That's where you should have left it. You arsehole,' I screamed at him gritting my teeth, willing the itching to stop. They both stood there like frightened rabbits caught in the blinding light of an express train.

'Are you going to tell the police?' Laura whined softly.

'I'll wait until I see the damage to the car.'

'That could be weeks John. Please don't say anything. I can't stand the suspense, it's torture,' Iain said.

'Neither of you know what torture is. You…you pair of…Torture! You know nothing about torture.' The angrier I became the more intense was the itching along my legs. 'Not being able to scratch my FN legs. That's FN torture.' I screamed at them.

Let Us Fly to Paris

The postman was coming and Aisha's heart began to race. She jumped off the swing and ran. She had to meet him before he could deliver the letters. Would he tell anyone, if she received a Valentine's?

Last year she hung her card in her bedroom window for the whole world to see, the red ribbons, the roses and declaration of eternal love. They sentenced her to twenty lashes that would save her innocence from the evils of seduction. Mother cried to take the blame so they whipped her. Father cried for the 150 ringgits he paid for cream and bandages.

Aisha checked that her hijab covered her designer jeans. She pulled her scarf over her head and neck in case her sultry red lace inflamed the postman's dignity. She bowed her head. His hold lingered for contact over the gate as she gripped the letters for her father and a small brown parcel. She bowed her head again and stared at his feet. He gave the bundle a tug, but Aisha held on and just stared at the ground. He muttered something about the intensive heat and the Monsoon weather, before he let go and left.

It was sensible of Pascal to wrap their secret in brown paper. Hidden like her emotions growing wildly in her dreams. Amongst the travel books in the library he had whispered about going to Europe. They would climb the Eiffel Tower and kiss. That's what they did in Paris and no one cared because you were in love. Poor Pascal, he has yet to climb the garden gate. How will our feelings ever go beyond the magnolia trees that grow inside the garden wall?

Aisha sat on the swing with the parcel on her lap, to and fro. What's the point of roses and ribbons; what's the point of words of love, what's the point? What use is happiness locked in a cupboard, wrapped in paper? Aisha pulled the string loose and unwrapped the box.

Two white doves where held in a net, they shivered and blinked in the daylight. How cruel. Each had a ring, on one of their legs, printed with a name. Two doves called Aisha and Pascal. Inside was a note.

Her mother heard Aisha's screams and came running into the garden. The doves flew past her head to the top branches of the magnolia tree, where they sat bobbing. Free. On the swing Aisha was flying high, back and forwards. She laughed and then slipped off the seat and jumped onto the ground.

'What is it Aisha?' Her mother grabbed her hands. 'Why are you laughing? Not so loud.'

'Look at the doves Mother, look in the tree.'

'Shoo shoo.' Her mother waved her kitchen cloth and the doves flew off. 'There now, they've gone.'

'Fly, you little doves, fly.' Aisha waved to the birds. 'They left a note, Mother. Read this.'

"Let us be free, let us fly to Paris".

The Flower Girl

I promised to come for Sunday afternoon tea on my mother's birthday. Yes of course you know I'll be there, I told Aunt Mary, and yes I'll bring a present, it would be a pleasant surprise for her.

My mother is not easy to surprise and usually it is me who is caught unaware as she entertains everyone with yet another story from my childhood. For the last few years I just bought her a card and took along a chocolate cake from the supermarket. This year will be different.

There was excitement in my mother's eyes as she dashed across the hall. Her floral dress swept behind as if in a slipstream flapping as a sail would in a gust of wind. In her wake Aunt Mary bobbed behind. I stood at the front door with a girl, who lifted the bundles of flowers out towards my mother now hurling at us with her arms stretched wide. I am no longer the little child she insists I still am, but I daren't speak. I waited for my mother's sloppy kiss. With both arms wrapped around a potted dwarf conifer and a box of Black Magic chocolates tucked in the foliage, I hoped to escape her embrace and usual greeting of; how's my little baby darling. I didn't, she managed to claw the plant to one side.

To her I will always be that little baby, the one who cried when she fed the chickens. She tells the story so vividly as with all her other anecdotes about my childhood. I often wonder if they are really true. The only recollections I have are of her versions told at family gatherings, where I can only laugh when I hear her new embellishments.

Apparently on that day, the morning sky was a brilliant blue and clouds floated like great bundles of cotton wool. My mother was feeding the chickens and she threw corn around, casting it over the dry ground. I was amongst the hens and they pecked around my tiny feet, I had stumbled and sat on the ground. She threw some grains and I caught a handful then chewed and spat them out. My mother had laughed and wiped my mouth. Now don't eat the corn or you'll grow fat like the cockerels she had said, and then Grandpa will have you for Sunday dinner. When Grandpa had visited the next day, I'd hung onto her leg and cried.

She snatched the bundle of flowers from the girl at the door and thrust them onto Aunt Mary.

'Kitchen Mary, there're a few vases somewhere.' She took hold of the girl in a grasping hug then gently stroked her face. 'How young and soft without a blemish. It was sensible not to wear makeup,' she said, 'and such lovely hair.' She combed her hand over the girl's head. 'Not to worry, you can borrow one of my brushes.'

She took a firm hold of the girl's hand and led her into the dining room where the chatter stopped and the gathered family all turned to look. I put the conifer pot down on a side table behind the door.

'Not there, oh dear, Mary come and get this plant. Put it somewhere,' my mother shouted and turned to the assembled family. 'Listen everyone. This is, sorry, what's your name?'

'Emma,' said the girl.

'Look everyone, this is Emma,' my mother announced to the staring faces around the dining table.

'Isn't she lovely?' Emma blushed as my mother pushed her forward. 'You can sit here next to Granny.'

I was directed down to the other end of the table where Uncle George sat, apparently he wasn't feeling well. I watched my Grandmother take Emma's hand and heard the last few words.

'… I do have bothers and sisters,' Emma said.

'Now that's enough Granny,' my mother interrupted. 'They're not married yet.'

I saw Emma squirm and glance around uncomfortably as everyone chuckled and nodded. They offered her the ham sandwiches, sponge cake and millionaires' shortbread all at the same time.

'Yes tuck in and eat up,' they chorused.

Aunt Mary came from the kitchen and poured the tea. Emma fidgeted with a napkin and politely ate what was offered. She did tuck in and appeared to enjoy the food, but shifted awkwardly in her chair in response to the haphazard interrogations about her life.

'Do you swim Emma?' My mother smiled at her.

I cringed. Clearly a prelude to one of her childhood stories told for the amusement of everyone at my expense.

We were on a family picnic by the Logan stream where mothers sat, gossiping, on woollen rugs. The ducks had given up on gratuitous crusts and equally bored I had wandered off. At six years old I became the invincible Harrison Ford determined to retrieve the sunken treasure from the bottom of the pool in the stream. On my third attempt to reach the imaginary gold I snagged my trunks on a root. My thrashing around in the water attracted a rescue party of aunts and curly haired cousins, who looked on, all engulfed in hysterical laughter. Now the incident about my bare bottom has been added to my mother's volume of embarrassing tales and suitably exaggerated with the addition of my dingle dangle scaring the ducks.

It turns out that Emma swims for the Hamilton water Polo team and this distracted my mother.

I helped Uncle George pour some more tea.

'No milk,' he said. Instead he covertly tipped in a golden liquid from a small hip flask.

'Come and see my paintings.' My mother stood. She took hold of Emma's hand, and pulled her into the hall heading towards her art studio.

I followed them to rescue Emma from my mother's enthusiasm, especially over my childish paintings that she still keeps on her studio wall. My infant hand paintings, drawings of garden birds and my masterpiece of a three-legged horse are part of her conducted tour to visitors. Why couldn't they have gone from the fridge door into oblivion or into a forgotten scrapbook that might collect dust in the attic?

'I really need to go back to work.' Emma said and stood firm in the hall. 'Thank you for the tea and it was nice to meet you.' She hurried off and closed the front door before my mother could stop her.

'Well.' She turned to me. 'What a really nice girl? Don't you think she was rather rude, rushing off like that?'

'Mum, do you like the presents of flowers and chocolate. Were you surprised?'

'Yes well, Emma was certainly a surprise. You must bring her again.'

'Mother, I have no idea who Emma is or anything about her. She just helped to carry the flowers from the shop.'

'She's a flower girl. Oh dear. Surely you can do better.' She turned and went into the kitchen. 'Mary come on, lets have some fresh tea for everyone.'

Martha.

The doctor placed one hand on Martha's shoulder and lifted her chin with the other. She swept his hand away and stared at him. He gave her a large paper tissue and gestured to the nurse, standing nearby, to come forward.

'I'm sorry Martha. Really I am so sorry. The nurse will help you.' The doctor turned and walked away.

Martha pushed past them, she wanted to scream but a lump in her throat constricted and contained her grief. She ran out of the room, down the stairs and through the hospital exit into the freezing dark morning. She gasped in the frosty air and exhaled the stale hospital odour that had collected in her lungs. Condensation rose from the hot tears pouring down her cheeks. She needed to get away and go somewhere else, to walk, to be alone and scream for vengeance, to vent her anger at the world for the injustice of it all. Why, why her?

The salt and gravel strewn on the path crunched beneath her footsteps and the sound echoed around the cold sandstone buildings. Following the street downhill, she wandered up the steps that led over the expressway bridge; she shivered and pulled her coat tight. She gripped at the railing of the footbridge and looked down onto the road of frosted tarmac.

'Why, O why,' she screamed. Crows disturbed from their perch in nearby trees responded with a chorus of caws. A lone car passed under the bridge, its driver unaware that it was tears and not rain drops that speckled the windscreen. She looked back towards the York Hill hospital with its tall prominent chimney that released a continuous white plume of smoke skywards as if releasing the remains of incinerated souls.

'Why are you so cruel,' she shouted and looked upwards at the low morning sky. 'You have her now,' Martha whispered. The clouds spread as a grey blanket over the city, and indifferent to the inhabitants either still asleep or starting their journeys to work. With her back to the hospital she walked on towards the river, she walked and she talked.

'It's my fault; no children and he always told me. Always telling me.' She looked up at the cyclist rushing past, but he wasn't listening.

'No one cares. I saw you Susan and I loved you straight away. The adoption was so perfect,' she said. 'But still he left us,' she shouted. A foraging blackbird, disturbed by her outburst, cocked its head sympathetically before flying off to search in some bushes further away and where it was quieter.

Martha stopped and spoke, 'its over now, no one cares.'

As if the motionless river trapped by a thin layer of ice was listening,

The dark sheen on the water reflected the lights from the BBC building opposite, where they read the World's news, but not her news. She moved on and in the background the beginning of traffic sounds were muffled between the low clouds and the blanket of snow, her footsteps creaked loudly.

'Leukaemia,' she spoke quietly. 'O Susan you were only four. School next year.' The joggers' sidestepped to avoid her. 'They lied. They said it would be OK. Why you.' She sobbed. 'I loved you so much.' Another wave of tears erupted and rolled down her face.

'What have I to cry about,' she spoke louder, 'no one cries any more.'

Bypassing her the anonymous people, hidden in heavy coats with their heads wrapped in woollen scarves and hats, did not want to listen as they rushed away to the footbridge and crossed over the Clyde. She walked past the taxi drivers waiting for fares, smoking and huddling outside the towering hotel. They gave her a quick glance then turned back to read their newspapers. She walked on, and saw herself as a lone sad figure reflected in the windows of the hotel restaurant.

'You were so small, so beautiful, so happy,' she mumbled.

Looking out from behind the hotel window, a young man in a business suit momentarily watched her then turned his attention away to drink his steaming coffee.

'The owl and the pussycat went to sea. You sang. So sweet, you knew every word.' She let out a sobbing wail and wandered on.

The orange streetlights switched off in unison and, with crunching footsteps on the snow, rushing shadows pushed and passed her by in the monochromatic gloom. She carried on oblivious to the people making their way to work and walked along the pavement next to the main road over the river.

'How am I to live without you? How I need you.' Martha stared down into the grey water below. The ice was breaking up creating spaces like doors opening with a welcoming invitation. Behind her the vehicles creeping over Skew Bridge slowed and crawled as the traffic increased, and the noise became louder.

'How I miss you,' she shouted above the din and into the exhaust smoke swirling around her.

A hand grabbed hold of her arm and she turned and saw a familiar face.

'Martha. Here you are,' the woman said in a soft voice. 'I've found you.'

'Margaret!' Martha threw her arms tightly around her sister and with convulsive shaking sobbed loudly into her coat.

'I know about Susan. I'm so sorry Martha. I'm so sorry. Come on, I'm taking you home.'

Made in the USA
Charleston, SC
25 April 2015